HURRICANE KISS

HURRICANE KISS

KISS

DEBORAH BLUMENTHAL

Albert Whitman & Company
Chicago, Illinois

Also by Deborah Blumenthal

The Lifeguard

Mafia Girl

A Different Me

Special thanks to Tom Krause for his guidance on protecting student-athletes from time demands of overzealous coaches.

Library of Congress Cataloging-in-Publication data is on file with the publisher.

Text copyright © 2016 by Deborah Blumenthal
Published in 2016 by Albert Whitman & Company
ISBN 978-0-8075-3448-9 (hardcover)
ISBN 978-0-8075-3450-2 (paperback)
Printed in the United States of America
10 9 8 7 6 5 4 3 2 1 BP 25 24 23 22 21 20 19 18 17 16

Design by Ellen Kokontis
Cover and interior photos © isitsharp/iStock, John Finny/Getty Images

For more information about Albert Whitman & Company,
visit our web site at www.albertwhitman.com.

To the memory of the estimated 1,833 women, men, and children who lost their lives during Hurricane Katrina

PROLOGUE

JILLIAN

My room is dark, except for the glow of the TV. I'm about to change the channel when the weather report comes on. Something—either the subtle change in the meteorologist's tone or the turbulence of the swirling neon-colored fields on the Doppler weather map—sets off a panic inside me. I shut off the TV and pull the covers over my head, trying to calm myself in my blanket tent.

But as I fall asleep, I see massive fields of darkness closing off the sky. The trees begin to pulsate wildly, sending out high-pitched whirring vibrations that send chills down my spine. They seem to signal an ominous warning from another planet. The clouds grow heavier after sucking oxygen from the universe, dooming us to suffocation. It feels like cosmic punishment for some great human wrongdoing. I search for someone, anyone, to go to for help, but no one is there. I'm all alone on an open, winding road that dead-ends somewhere in an open field.

I wake up gasping for air, as if I were being asphyxiated in a car with the engine running inside a locked garage, unable to free myself. It takes forever for my heart to slow down.

I don't tell anyone about my nightmare the next morning, especially not my mom. She'd blame it on stress from school. Only it's not. School in Texas is easy compared to my classes in New York. And my friends? Your imagination is running wild, they'd say. Take yoga, do deep-breathing. Talk to a shrink.

What makes it worse is that the next night the dream comes back, like a night-blooming primrose waiting for darkness to unfurl again, delivering the same message of doom.

RIVER

Monster storm, monster storm, monster storm. The words vibrate in my head and the panic surges up so hard and fast it chokes off the back of my throat. A wild grab for the bottle in the dark sends it flying, pills scattering everywhere. I drop to the floor, frantically scooping them up, swallowing one, and then another, to get me through the night.

PART 1

URGENT—NATIONAL WEATHER SERVICE UPDATE, HOUSTON, TX

Hurricane Danielle could pack winds at the upper range of category 5… over 150 mph…once hurricane force onset…do not venture outside!… devastating damage expected…much of the region will be uninhabitable for weeks…wood-framed structures will be destroyed. Concrete block garden apartments will sustain major damage…high-rise office and apartment buildings will sway and could collapse. Flying debris will be widespread…even heavy items such as vehicles may be airborne. High winds and debris will be deadly for people, pets, and livestock in the open. Power will be out for weeks. Water shortages will be widespread.

Evacuate by all available escape routes.

CHAPTER 1

24 HOURS TO LANDFALL

JILLIAN

River and his dad are waiting for me. I have to get out my duffel. I have to pack. Only I'm paralyzed. What do I do? What do I take?

Take only what's essential. That's the mantra on TV and radio.

Clothes? Favorite books? Cubby, the teddy bear I've had since I was three? The tiny red silk pouch with my baby teeth?

All over our city two million people must be asking themselves the same question, but that doesn't make it easier. I've never run from a category five hurricane before. There's no rule book. No self-help guide. To make it more unreal, the sky is now Popsicle blue. No storm clouds or distant thunder. No ominous warnings above us. Has everyone lost it?

Our neighborhood is carpeted with neon green grass and turquoise swimming pools. Dogs bolting from fenced-in backyards and kids tripping on sidewalks make headlines. Nothing bad happens here.

Only everything is about to change.

"Jillian," my mom says, suddenly appearing in my doorway, "let's go!"

But she's not going anywhere. I'm the one leaving. Without her. The familiar fear courses through me.

"Why can't I stay *with* you?" I ask for the eightieth time. "Or at least go with Ethan."

"I'm going with Jerry," Ethan shouts from his bedroom. "And we don't want you anyway." Typical Ethan. Forever excluding his little sister.

"Ethan," my mom says, in warning.

"Lowlife," I yell back.

"I have to work, you know that," she says, tired of going over this again. "And I want you out of harm's way." Then her face softens. "Do you really think I want to be here when the storm hits?"

Um, yes, Mom, I think you do. Disasters make good copy. She could get a Pulitzer out of this one.

If she survives to write it.

If any of us are left to read it.

"Tomorrow's Astros game was canceled," Ethan says, in a tone that sounds like someone died. My brother is on the phone with his separated-at-birth best friend, Jerry.

"Who cares?" I say. "Lupe Tortilla is closed." How will I survive without my weekly fix of fiery shrimp tacos and refried black beans? Or my watermelon Slurpees from the 7-Eleven? Dominos, the only holdout, is still delivering, but for how long?

I yank out my duffel and then kick it aside. I reach for a blood red nail polish called Tomboy No More, like giving myself a pedicure now makes sense. Like anything does.

"Jillian," my mom says passing my doorway again, pens and notebooks in her hands. She ignores the unmade bed and the clothes scattered on the floor, because things like that don't matter anymore.

But she does a double take and stares at my toes. "I cannot believe you're…please, let's *go*."

One body-bag-sized bag to hold my life: money, snacks, jeans, T-shirts, and random possessions from my almost seventeen-year-old life balled up inside.

"We should *both* go!"

She comes closer, pushing my mop of red hair out of my face.

"You have gorgeous blue eyes," she says. "Why do you hide them?"

"I don't *hide* them."

"I love you," she says, her face softening. "Let's not go over this again. I'm a reporter. It's my job to be here."

It's like she refuses to accept how bad it could get. Google "cat 5 storms" and what do you find? Sustained winds of over 157 miles an hour. Storm surges greater than eighteen feet above normal. They used to be rare. Not anymore. Between 2000 and 2009 alone, there were eight. And now there's Danielle.

But my mom's not paying attention to my pleading. I'm invisible to her. Orphaned. My single parent, career-woman mom is committed to succeeding in her job, whatever the stakes. Her mind is made up. All morning she's been plotting strategy with her office. She's renting a truck instead of using her car. She's pulled waders out of her closet, only now she's not going trout fishing in Montana with her book group. Waders will come in handy crossing streets flooded with waist-high water. She's stocked up on enough dry food for a moon landing, not to mention a dozen topped-off red plastic fuel cans, because gas will run out while mobs of cars on the freeway escape in one direction: O-U-T.

The plan is for the press to bunk at an office building off the freeway where the mayor and his staff will set up headquarters and monitor the storm. So while other families are leaving together, my mom will be staying behind.

And me?

I'm stuck in the backseat of my next-door neighbor's SUV to fend for myself. Just me with Mr. Harlan Daughtry, a big oil VP, and his son, River. Me in the back. River in the front. Almost as close as the night of the school's full-moon picnic.

The night he kissed me, rocking my world.

A lifetime ago.

• • •

Tall and blond with a body that makes smart girls stupid, that's River. What's changed since last year is that his cocky grin has been replaced by a wary coolness. But the biggest difference is in his eyes.

They don't meet mine anymore.

I don't know much about him now, not unless you count the rumors. No surprise about that. The star quarterback gets expelled without warning, so people talk. And whisper.

But none of us knows the real story. And he's not talking.

I can't help wondering what happened. He had it all. He was smart and popular. He carried the team. What could he have done that was so terrible that overnight he got cuffed and thrown into the back of a police car, ending up in a juvie prison in the West Texas desert?

RIVER

I upend my backpack, sending school garbage clattering to the floor, and then jam it with essentials for exile.

Shit.

The T-shirt drawer is sticking.

I wedge out the old school newspaper stuck behind it. Me on the front page.

While at 6'3" River Daughtry is the perfect drop-back quarterback, when you can run 4.40 in the forty, you can play any position in the field.

Daughtry has a special innate quality that surpasses strength and speed, that surpasses self-confidence. He burns with raw power and invincibility.

Hard to recognize the picture. Tangled hair falling in my face, stripes of eye black, like war paint, and a smug grin as I hoist up the trophy. It hurts just to look at me then. Everything was so different. My fairy-tale life. I remember Carla, my girlfriend in LA, eyeing the picture. It was right before we moved from LA to Houston.

"You look hot, River," she said, laughing.

The me that doesn't exist anymore.

The world of before.

Drop-kicked from the Ivy League track in Houston and then thrown into that West Texas snake pit that eroded my brain. My hands shake as I reach into my pocket for the orange plastic bottle, my lifeline to sanity, and toss a pill down my throat.

Take only what's essential.

My mom's picture, clothes. What am I forgetting? What? The list. Where's my list? My brain's fried from the psych drugs they pushed down my throat. I can't remember things anymore. I go to the corkboard target on my wall and pull out a knife. I slip it into my back pocket.

"River, you almost ready?" shouts my dad.

Not even close. "Almost."

To make matters worse, Jillian will be along for the ride, all sweet perfume and memories, taking me back to where I refuse to go. Just seeing her reminds me of the me I'll never be again, the weight of the past like a boot crushing the back of my neck.

Screw the past, screw everything.

CHAPTER 2

JILLIAN

Just a week ago today, everything seemed almost normal. It was before the forecast changed from blue skies to black clouds and imminent disaster. It was only September, but I'd been consumed with studying, obsessing about my grade point average. I was preoccupied with the months ahead when I'd be applying to colleges and writing essays. Essays to make ordinary me magically stand out from the competition. Essays that required me to weigh in on what I thought about pivotal events in my lame life, or someone else's. Essays that asked me to describe ethical dilemmas I faced and how I handled them.

Seriously, why did I have to be held under a microscope to see if the way my mind worked meshed with some admissions board's exalted criteria? My life was my life. Weren't grade points enough to go on?

Lunch was usually a welcome break from obsessing about college. So I went out to meet Kelly. Instead of eating in the lunch hall, we liked to eat outside under the canopy of giant live oak trees. I got there first. As I waited for Kelly, I noticed Coach Briggs, his ramrod straight posture, eyes laser focused ahead, strutting toward the football field. And then that got me thinking of River and how his life imploded near the end of last year, our sophomore year.

I'd been attracted to River, but who wasn't? Sometimes I thought it was mutual, but other times I laughed at the idea. River was comfortable in his own skin, easygoing, flirty with everybody. That went along with being the star football player, Harrison High's hot Prince Charming, having your pick of girls, like a rock star who amuses himself by playing musical beds, not concerned with breaking hearts. Besides, I had Aidan.

"You're lost in thought," Kelly said, dropping down next to me. I hadn't even noticed her coming out to our lunch spot. "What were you thinking about? You looked sad," she said.

I told her I'd been thinking about River.

"You see him much?"

"I ran into him the other night when we were both taking out the trash. He had a sweatshirt on, the hood pulled up. He barely nodded."

I didn't tell her what else I'd seen recently. River's room is across the yard from mine. When the windows are open, I hear his guitar. Ever since he came back he plays for hours at a time.

But a few nights ago, a dull, steady pounding had woken me.

The sound was coming from River's window. *Thud. Thud. Thud. Thud. Thud.*

Like fists on a punching bag. I wondered if he was beating someone up. I got out of bed and walked to the window, but all I could see was the flickering light of a TV in the darkness.

In the morning I headed for his backyard gate after he and his dad left. I had to know what the sound was. I tiptoed along the narrow walkway, jelly-bean-sized pebbles crunching under my feet. I stopped at River's window. An unmade bed, clothes and towels dropped everywhere. Over on the far wall, by a huge TV, was a target. Only River didn't use darts. It was covered with slender knives, each suspended by the tips of their gleaming silver blades, all piercing the bull's eye.

I stared at the knives. That was a side of River I hadn't seen before. Was he angry? About what?

"Jillian? You're someplace else."

"Sorry, what?"

"What's River doing now?" Kelly asked.

"He's a stock boy at Whole Foods, I think. That's his life, except for running. He must do marathons all the time." I unwrapped my tuna salad sandwich and then tossed it aside. "What does someone have to do to get expelled and sent to juvie prison?"

"Not jaywalking," she said. "Heavy stuff like murder, robbery, dealing drugs, rape, arson."

Everyone in school had their own theory about what happened to River, but the truth never came out. The school wanted it buried, so they never issued any information to us. "I thought I knew him."

"Maybe nobody knew him," she said. "People snap, they get mad. Who knows? Or they're just unlucky. Wrong place, wrong time, whatever."

"Unlucky," I said. "I'll go with that."

Just then I looked up and saw Lexie, the head cheerleader, walking past us. Tight red T-shirt. Short denim skirt with a black widow spider tattoo above her ankle. She glanced over at me with a self-satisfied expression.

"Bitch," she mouthed.

I turned away, my hand closing around Aidan's ring. I wore it on a chain around my neck. I had a steady boyfriend I could count on. He was dependable. Trustworthy. He would never fall for someone like Lexie, who worked her way up the ladder of players on the team, finally latching onto River, the star at the top.

11

So what if River had kissed me like no one ever had? It was one kiss. One moment in time. And then it was over. Everyone crushed on River. Anyway, last semester's picnic was history. Lexie and River were history. I had to stop obsessing about the past.

But old habits die hard.

23 HOURS TO LANDFALL

I was obsessing about the past. I had to stop. That was a week ago. Ancient history. Now the clock was ticking. Only twenty-three hours to landfall. No time to think about anything except getting out and staying alive.

I snap into action, studying what's in my closet. Flip-flops? Sneakers? I think about flooded streets. What if the bayou overflowed and poisonous snakes floated out? Copperheads, cottonmouths—your standard-issue Texas nightmare—nothing to worry about there. I read they don't make as much anti-venom these days. I drag my tall boots from the back of my closet, but they weigh a ton, so I throw them back.

Take only what's essential.

I go into Ethan's room. "What are you taking?"

"Music and guitars," he says, yanking CDs off a bookshelf without turning to me.

Right. "What about Jerry?"

"Some six packs."

What did I expect?

I zip my stuffed duffle, then a second later unzip it to switch out a royal blue T-shirt for a navy one because when outrunning a hurricane you should definitely obsess about the hues of blues and, God, yes, I'm freaking, I am. I drop-kick the bag downstairs and out to the driveway where I stuff it into Harlan's trunk. River, in the front seat, ignores me, and I ignore him back.

RIVER

The hard-assed ex-marine wedges carton after carton into the trunk, packed as tightly as cemented bricks. Files, water bottles, a flashlight, and finally a white metal box with a red cross on it. I wonder where he stashed his prized uniform, embalmed in plastic, from the hall closet.

The only holdout, my guitar. No music in his life. Too healing, or whatever.

"There's no room, River." He holds a stiff arm out to me.

I grab the guitar away and wedge it into the backseat against the door. "How hard was that?"

He doesn't answer.

Coexistence. The sum total of our relationship. Since my mom died, we sleep in the same house, eat at the same table, but that's about...

Flash of red hair. She walks out of her house. A nanosecond glance at her through the rearview mirror, and then I look away. She stuffs her duffle into our trunk and goes back inside.

I don't want to be in the car with them.

I don't want to be leaving the city.

I don't want to be part of this.

No one holds cat 5 drills, because who thinks they'll ever happen? You can't cancel life for a day and tell an entire city to get lost. I max my music and shut my eyes.

Austin. They can wake me when we get to Austin.

JILLIAN

I start to get into the car and then stop. Wait. What am I doing? I'm losing it. I forgot something. What? I dash back into the house and look all around. My toothbrush, right. The phone rings. Kelly. I smile at the picture of her in a pink bikini with a floppy straw hat pulled down over one eye. I took it last year in Galveston when the surf was whisper-calm and people were out paddling their sea kayaks. It looked like a poster for a summer in paradise.

"I wish you could come with us," she says.

Zero chance of that. She's got two younger brothers, and her parents drive a midsize Honda. I stare out the window at River in the car. He's sitting there stock-still.

In a last-ditch effort to avoid going with River, I had asked my mom if I could ride on Kelly's roof rack. Her answer was no answer. It was Harlan's SUV for me. Friend of the family, ex-marine, so trustworthy, whatever.

"It's fine, Kel." I work to sound sincere, which is a reach. But Kelly knows; she's been my best friend since I moved to Texas from New York two years ago.

"Are you...nervous about being in the car with him?"

Yes, no, maybe so. I have no idea really. Does he make me nervous? Not like seeing-a-snake-in-the-backyard nervous. Or getting-a-wisdom-tooth-pulled nervous. How many kinds are there? Does he make me anything now? I haven't been close enough to him in over a year to find out.

I walk to the window. He's still sitting there, right arm out the window, fingers drumming against the top of the car. I think about the knives. Did he pack them? Part of his essentials? Who or what will he target?

"Austin's less than three hours away, Kel. I'm not a baby, I can take care of myself."

"Mmm, but can you take care of him?" she says, with a pointed laugh. "Seriously, J. They don't send choir boys to juvie—"

"Kel—" There's a beep. "It's Aidan, call you back."

"This so sucks," Aidan says. "We're going to be stuck on the highway till next week."

"Aidan, it probably won't even—"

"—At least if we were together and you didn't have to go with that..." He makes a sound like something is stuck in his throat.

"Three hours is no big deal."

"Yeah...not unless—"

"—What?"

"Whatever...nothing...call me when you get there, or anytime. I want to hear from you."

"Don't worry, Aidan."

"That's what boyfriends do," he mutters, and then he's gone.

I call Kelly back. "What did I forget to take?"

"Fav jeans, T-shirts, undies, deodorant, water, snacks, body, soul, and phone. Keep it together, BF," she says. "We'll all laugh about Danielle next week."

I spot my diary with the charm-sized lock. I write something in it every day, even if it's just a quirky line from a book or a smart quote:

Normal people are the ones you don't know very well.

Reality is wrong; dreams are for real.

Suffering introduces you to yourself and reminds you that you are not the person you thought you were.

Why that compulsion to write things down? Maybe fifty years from now I'll wake up with amnesia and want to know the history of me.

Ethan got me my first diary when I was eight—at least my mom wanted it to look that way because she wrote his name on the card in a squiggly babyish handwriting. My diary held everything important to eight-year-old me, from pictures of birthday cakes with purple sugar pansies to lists of people I'd invite to my party, and a special page devoted to my suckworthy dad.

I stuff it into my back pocket and slip on the silver charm bracelet with the heart, my junior-high graduation gift. I look at the inscription:

We're so proud of you! Love, Mom and Ethan.

"Mom..." I shout. "Anything else I need to..." I stop. The handyman is hammering plywood boards over the windows. The noise is deafening.

One nail at a time, our sunny house with the daffodil walls and the view of the crisscrossed jasmine vines over the picket fence is being converted into a dark, airless tomb.

"It's an old house, but it's solid," my mom insists. "It's survived hurricanes and tropical storms before."

Not a cat 5 hurricane! But I don't say that. She's not listening anymore.

"Jillian, you ready?" she shouts again, now from downstairs. Yes. No. I don't know.

"Almost."

I loved our house the moment I saw it. It has a glass wall facing the backyard pool, and upstairs, through the skylights, you can see the stars. Best of all, there's a ladder up to my private space in the attic. We call it the lair.

It's where I go to hide.

I stare at my stained-glass window decorations in Crayola colors sparkling in the sunlight, and my spidery dream catchers dangling from the bedposts. Native Americans believe that good dreams pass through the hole in the center, making their way from the feathers to the sleeping person, but bad ones get snared in the web, zapped by the morning sun. I slide a purple feathery dream catcher off the bed post and into my back pocket.

What if everything is gone when I get back? How do you start life over, without anything but memories?

I run down to the kitchen and stuff peanut-butter crackers and apple-juice boxes into my bag. No stopping at all if we don't have to. We're leaving later than we should have.

"After the first wave of traffic is gone, it should be easier going," Harlan told my mom. What everyone secretly hoped was that at the last minute, Danielle would change direction.

Wishful thinking.

The *Houston Chronicle*'s ominous banner headline this morning: DANIELLE. Nothing else mattered now.

The last issue of the school paper sits on my bureau. "Danielle is holding us in its crosshairs like a mad assassin," I'd written, going for attention-grabbing. "We stand by helplessly as it pumps itself up like a bully on steroids preparing to close in. It can still change course. The next forty-eight hours will tell."

RIVER

Five minutes. Ten. Where is she, already? Maybe a last call to her boyfriend, swearing undying love. I glance up at the blue sky. The guys at Whole Foods were probably right. This whole evacuation thing could be a joke.

"I'm staying put," one of my coworkers said. "If it gets bad we'll hole up in an interior room till it blows over."

"No way I'm running," said another. "I've lived here my entire life, and we've always been fine. This is nuts."

But not my dad. He was gutting the place, packing work stuff, tax returns, food for a year, whatever. I snap on the car radio.

"We're doing what's humanly possible to protect the citizens of this city. We can't predict how directly we'll be hit, but we do know the devastating effects of Hurricane Katrina, with eighteen hundred people killed, two hundred seventy-five thousand homes destroyed in Louisiana, and another sixty-five thousand in Mississippi and Alabama, leaving a great swath of humanity with nothing more than the clothes on their backs."

"Mr. Mayor, many consider Katrina a once-in-a-lifetime storm, insisting that it will never happen again in our lifetime. Are you overreacting by calling for an evacuation for Hurricane Danielle?"

"Not at all, John—"

I stab the button.

What do I remember most about Katrina? A single statistic: the destruction left behind could fill four hundred football fields, each fifty-feet high with debris. I flash back to my mom. How would she be taking this if she were here? Even if she were scared, she wouldn't show it. She had a way of making bad look good, or at least OK. For my sake.

"River," my dad yells. "Go see if Jillian's ready. We have to get moving."

Shit. I get out of the damn car and go up to her front door. It's open. I walk in and head for the kitchen, then *smack*, we slam into each other as she turns the corner.

"Ow! God, River!"

"Jesus, sorry!" I back off abruptly, feeling like an asshole. My heart amps up. After all this time…her scent…"We need to get going—*now*," I say, clenching my fists. "It's getting late."

"I'm ready, I'm ready, OK," she says, her eyes flashing.

I storm out the door and climb back into the car, blasting the music. On the road together for three hours, then we'll part ways. If all goes as planned.

JILLIAN

I try to catch my breath, unsteady on my feet. What just happened? It was so long ago…How could I still feel…

I lean back against the wall, thinking back to how it all started—his first day at school, sophomore year, just over a year ago.

The first thing I found out about River was that his wrists were bound with barbed wire. A strong arm reached out in front of me one morning, gallantly propping open the front door of the school. That didn't happen much during the morning rush. I glanced back to ID the white knight with the barbed-wire tattoos. That's when I found out the second thing about him.

He had wintergreen eyes.

I didn't know his name back then. All I knew was that he was my new next-door neighbor and that this was the first time I'd seen him at school. I also knew he didn't know yet that I lived next door. Don't ask me why, but that made me feel as though I held this power over him.

"Happen to know where the office is?" he asked me in a breathless whisper. I glanced down at the mirrored aviators dangling from the neck of his black T-shirt, sunlight flickering off them hypnotically.

"Yes."

A crooked grin lit up his face. "OK then, twenty questions?"

"I'll spare you," I said, rising to the coolness challenge. "Straight ahead, then left after the display case with the trophies."

He saluted with two fingers and then leaned closer. "My first day," he whispered, grazing my ear with his lips. He sauntered off and I stood there watching him until, *whomp!* I got slammed by a backpack as someone pushed past me in the doorway. I looked at my watch. Why was I standing there? I was late for class.

First days were a bummer. To make it worse, from first glance you got pegged as hot or not. Not that River had to worry.

When I saw him a day later, he didn't see me. He was leaving the cafeteria line with enough spaghetti and meatballs to end world hunger.

"Whoa, hello!" said Sari Nelson, spotting River from our lunch table. "But he knows he's something. Just look at the way he walks; you can always tell."

"Give him a break," I said. "He just—"

"—made football," Kelly said.

"How do you know?" Sari asked.

"Bethany heard the coach talking to one of his teachers," Kelly said. "He was this megastar quarterback and the MVP at his last school in LA, and they hated to lose him, but after his mom died his dad asked for a transfer."

19

"You know more than I do," I said, "and he's my next-door neighbor."

Silence.

"Why didn't you tell us, Jillian?" Sari asked.

"There's nothing to tell. A moving van was parked in front of the house next door one day, and then I saw him and his dad helping the guys carry in cartons."

Kelly nudged me. "Have you spoken to him? What's he like?"

I shook my head. "My mom went over to say hi. I never see him at home, so he must start first period and go to practice after school."

"Here's the game plan," Kelly said. "Bake him fudge brownies. You'll be the one-girl welcome wagon. Then we can invite him to party."

"Right."

"I mean it, he would just think you're being nice."

"They'd probably come out half-raw, and I'd poison him with salmonella," I said. "Maybe buy?"

"So bring him a keg," Sari said, "and invite us over."

"And get him thrown off the team before he even starts? Coach Briggs would wring my neck," I said. "Any other brilliant ideas?"

"You're the editor of the paper, Jillian, you're always digging up answers. Come up with something," Kelly said.

But I didn't have to, at least right then. The bell rang and we all got up to go. River went out the side door toward the football field, munching an apple. No wonder I didn't see him much. The team practiced six days a week. Football isn't a sport in Texas; it's a religion. The highest calling. If River could carry the team to the top, he was made for life.

All he had to do was show up. And play the game.

CHAPTER 3

20 HOURS TO LANDFALL

RIVER

I stare at our house. Will it withstand a beating? It looks solid, but who knows? Like an athlete, pinned down and unable to fight back.

"Let me see you fight now, hotshot. Well? C'mon!" He punches me again and again. This is my entrance exam. Fight back and get crippled, or take it.

"No more fight in you?" The warden spits in my face and walks away. *"I think you're learning."*

I squeeze my eyes shut, trying to erase every second of the three months I was locked up in that pit like an animal. I go back to the beginning, the innocent time, our first few weeks of living in Houston.

A lifetime ago.

Her mom invited us over for a barbecue. We accepted, but it felt strange doing the new neighbor thing. When we got there my dad went outside and had a drink with her mom.

"Jillian's in the kitchen," her mom said. "Maybe you can help her." She pointed the way.

She was making deviled eggs, whipping each egg yolk with mayo, like it mattered to her to do it right. I couldn't just sit there watching, so I offered to peel some eggs—only I ended up messing up the whites and getting shell everywhere, so instead I carried stuff out to the backyard and managed not to drop anything.

I wanted to grab a beer from the fridge to relax. When everything was ready, we finally did sneak out a beer and shared it. That helped. Then we shared a second one. It made her giddy, which was contagious. After dinner we went out to the pool. They had a waterslide. It felt like we were ten-year-olds, going belly up and then closing our eyes, trying to land inside some rubber inner tubes. After that she challenged me to Ping-Pong.

"You are so going to lose," she said, her eyes sparkling.

I did. First on purpose, but she was on to me.

"You let me," she said, annoyed. "Don't do that." I laughed and played harder the next game. She didn't need a handicap. I still lost. That didn't happen much.

I was ready to play more games with her. Any kind.

She was easy to talk to; she listened. She asked me all kinds of questions about LA, like she wanted to know everything about it, like she really cared. She knew how weird it felt to leave all your friends behind and start over, at the same time liking the idea of landing in a new place with no baggage. Life didn't give you many chances to start over.

"You can be anyone you want to be in a new place," she said. "At least for a while."

I didn't tell her about my mom or why we moved, but somehow I think she knew. I didn't see a dad around. I figured we both got shortchanged

22

when it came to parents. It had to be hard for her; it always was, no matter what happened.

Sure I was drawn to her. She was real, no pretenses. The red hair spilling over her shoulders definitely worked for me, and so did the intensity in those killer blue-violet eyes and the way they held mine when she talked. But more than that was her vulnerability. The crazy part was that she didn't seem to have a clue about how magnetic she was. That innocence and the way it crept up on you was hotter than anything.

Still, I pushed those thoughts aside. I was the new neighbor; she was being nice. That's how she was with people. Easygoing, natural. Real. Down to earth, unlike some girls.

But she was the girl next door, and only someone who was out of his mind would start up with a neighbor. Plus she had a boyfriend, and he made damn sure everyone knew it.

JILLIAN

I glance down at my phone. No text from Aidan. Hmm, not like him. I toss it into my bag. My backpack is jammed against my thigh, and there's a laundry-sized duffle next to it, so I'm air-bagged in place. I open my backpack and double-check everything. Money, ID, a toothbrush, aspirin, tissues, sunblock, and a few Xanax that I stole from my mom's medicine cabinet, in case I freak. I look at River. What are his essentials besides his phone and all of iTunes?

Harlan takes a pipe wrench from his garage and turns off the water valve in the street in front of the house. Then he shuts the gas. My mom runs out at the last minute.

"Safe trip," she says to all of us, holding her hands out like the Pope offering a blessing. She leans through the window and kisses me on the cheek, stopping momentarily to study my face.

I roll my eyes. "Stop, I'll be *fine*."

"Of course you will," she says, putting up a brave front. "You'll be back before you know it."

Who is she reassuring?

"Call me as soon as you get to Linda's. We'll have a celebration when all of this is over."

"Whatever."

Linda has been my mom's friend since kindergarten. She lives in a brick townhouse in Austin that she swears is hurricane-proof.

"No worries," Harlan says, locking his seat belt. "We could live off what's in this car for a week if we had to."

"I owe you," she says, a tense smile on her face. "Phone charged?" she chirps for the millionth time as he backs out of the driveway.

I hate good-byes. Always have, always will. They're pathetically sad. There's so much that's unsaid. Unknown. And you know you shouldn't think those big, possibly terrible things that you're thinking, but you do anyway because you can't not, so the best thing to do is say good-bye fast and disappear.

No long portal good-byes, my mom always says.

Her face is in full view one moment and then poof, it vanishes, and all I'm left with is a picture in my head.

I'm not a total baby. This isn't the first time I've left home. There was Washington, DC, for a week-long school trip. There was sleep-away camp in Massachusetts for eight weeks, the entire summer session. I was OK with it; I survived, not counting the first two nights in the bunk.

But this is different.

What if we get hit dead on? What if their worst predictions come true?

Will my mom survive? Will Ethan? Will I have a family to come back to? A home? When you're down to one parent...

Don't think about the unthinkable, someone said. I try that.

24

It'll be fine. That will be my mantra. *It'll be fine.*

Then I remind myself to breathe.

RIVER

Stuck in the passenger seat like dead weight, watching someone else drive. I hate that. Especially when it's my dad behind the wheel. He goes slower when I'm next to him, like he's doing a demo of how to drive. It makes me nuts. Is there a reason he is now doing thirty instead of the pathetic forty he could? To jump-start the trip, he takes the shortcuts, going on local roads. Traffic is lighter than normal.

"So far, so good," he says. Right, tough navigation, sir, like he's kept the men under his watch alive on a jungle road with land mines.

"Looks like our timing was perfect," Jillian says.

"Don't be so sure," I say.

Not what I expected, at least so far. Did we manage to avoid the crowds? Everything looks the same, except the landscapers' flatbed trucks are gone now. No roar of lawn mowers or leaf blowers spewing gas fumes, keeping life all tidy. It's freaky calm.

I sit back. The pill has finally kicked in. The guy who invented these should get the Peace prize. I can breathe, for a while.

JILLIAN

Being in the backseat rewinds my head back to when I was six and Ethan and I had a dad. A dad who acted like one until the novelty wore off and he bailed because he was a total asshole. He and my mom would take us on road trips, and they'd dream up games to keep us from getting bored and fighting in the backseat.

"Take out your pens and write down the word, reincarnation, then tell me how many words you can make out of it." Or, "I want each of you to watch the road and find a hundred red cars," he'd say, dead serious.

We jumped at the bait. I'd sit there eyes fixed on the cars, determined to count every red one that passed, or meet another cosmic challenge like searching for license plates from every state. Ethan always tried to one-up me. I never believed it when he said he saw Alaska.

"Where?" I'd demand, and he'd laugh in my face.

"You didn't see it? It passed already. You missed it! You're too slow!"

"Liar, liar, pants on fire," I'd yell. But, deep down, I did believe him. He was my older brother, and I looked up to him.

I'd never admit it, but I still do.

The games must have worked because I was consumed with listing all the license plates I saw in a spiral notebook, so I felt like a real reporter.

Now the only plates I see are from Texas and Oklahoma. People from everyplace else had the brains to stay away. I stare at an Oklahoma plate: a lone Native American with a bow and arrow, taking aim at the wide-open sky. Something about that. I have to look away.

We coast along smoothly, the tinted windows cutting the glare. Finally Harlan turns and pulls onto the 290 entrance ramp to Austin so we can avoid the traffic lights. Smooth sailing and then...

Endless gridlock.

The entire highway is nearly at a standstill, traffic stretching from here to the horizon. The next thing I expect to see is someone pulling out sleeping bags and setting up a tent.

"Jesus," River says.

We stand still, inch forward every few seconds, and stop again.

"Is it the number of cars, or is something wrong up ahead?" I ask.

"Can't tell," Harlan says.

"Is there anyplace to call for information?"

He shakes his head.

"Yeah, 911," River says. "Tell them we are not cool with this. We want to be airlifted out."

"You're a big help," I say.

"Right."

I try to Google the local news station and put in "traffic tie-up on 290," but there's no report on what's holding things up. Then I go to the radio station. Still no news. There are helicopters flying above us. Why are there no traffic reports telling us what's causing this? Is anyone monitoring it? Are they even aware of what's happening?

No flashing lights or roadwork signs either. People are getting out of their cars and shrugging their shoulders, exchanging words with neighbors and trying to come to terms with the massive jam we're all part of. Half an hour, maybe more goes by and more people are outside their cars than in. A woman three cars ahead takes her miniature white poodle out of the car. She waits while he lifts his leg against the tire, and then puts him back inside.

"We'll be where she is in another hour," River says.

"Great," I say.

Harlan opens all the windows and cuts the engine. Sweat beads on my forehead. And no, lame brain me did not include zit cream in her *essentials* bag. Or whoa, not even Tampax, I now realize, and I'm not even sure when my period is due because I forgot my calendar, so genius me might as well throw herself out of the car and die now, saving Danielle the trouble.

I stare at the back of River's head. Not that he has to worry about zits or periods, and he can pee at the side of the road without searching for heavy cover. He rubs the back of his neck, and then maxes his music. I feel the vibrations inside me.

18 HOURS TO LANDFALL

RIVER

I put my headphones on and blast my brain with music, not that it changes anything.

I'm not roasting.

I didn't forget the second bottle of goddamn pills.

I'm not imprisoned in a packed car.

I'm not powerless to change anything, like a guy who got railroaded by a sick system of criminal *injustice* that puts your head in a vise and laughs when you scream from the pain.

Live inside your head instead of the real world, the damn shrinks say. *Change your perceptions. Pretend.* Pretend. *Pretending something can actually make it happen*, they insist. *If you believe hard enough.* Believe? Hope? Those words aren't in my vocabulary anymore. What I go with now is reality. Cold, hard, reality: what's right smack in front of me.

I sit back as music fills my insides like a survival potion.

CHAPTER 4

JILLIAN

I stare at River's profile as he gazes out the window. Jaw set stoically, with steely resolve. I can't help thinking about how much he's changed in less than a year.

It had to have been football. Something to do with the demands of the game. He probably slept no more than four hours a night back when he was on the team. That was enough to make anyone crazy. Then there were the pressures of school and the need to keep your grades up to stay on the team, as well as for college apps the following year.

He had no mom to cook or care for him, just a woman who cleaned once a week and then drove off. And every day he was pushed by a coach who had only one thing on his mind—victory for the team. Failure wasn't an option. It reflected badly on the coach; it would mean that he failed. And Coach Briggs didn't do failure.

Did he push River too far? Everybody has a breaking point. I heard rumors about drugs, about punishments, like making the players run extra miles when they screwed up.

What happened to him? What did he do? Did he snap? Why hadn't the story come out?

What scared me most was when someone whose dad was a cop said that Briggs had an order of protection against River.

That meant he was a real threat. It meant he was violent.

RIVER

The big guns are here with us. Doom on the horizon? I can thank my dad for moving us to Texas. For uprooting me from the best high school in LA, opening the way for all the shit that rained down on my head.

I shift in my seat, jammed in, a cooler hogging most of the space by my feet. I kick it away and try to stretch, but end up smacking the roof of the car.

"Take it easy," my dad says, staring ahead.

"If I could friggin' move here, I would."

As usual, the world is closing in on me. On the radio someone is interviewing the head of the animal shelter.

"For category 3 storms and above we evacuate the shelters," he says. "Air-conditioned trucks are already in transit, taking our dogs and cats to shelters in Dallas and Austin where they'll be safe."

Trapped. I picture them caged up in the vans, imprisoned. Scared, homeless, not knowing where they're going or why. No one to comfort them.

The memories flood back. I was staring out the window one day at the center and saw a stray dog amble by, his head down, desperately hunting for food. I wanted to call it over, to comfort it, but why give it hope? If one of the guards heard me, he'd probably shoot it just for spite and then laugh about it. Nothing was sacred there. Nothing and no one.

Briggs could have worked there—he was just like them. He didn't give a shit about anyone or anything. Except maybe his canary, which I never quite got.

I always loved dogs. I begged for one when I was a kid. Big, small, brown, black, white, anything, I didn't care what it looked like. I didn't care if it had four legs or two eyes; I just wanted a dog of my own. Silent, loving, devoted, all mine. There were so many of them just abandoned, locked in crappy cages, depressed, desperate for human contact. I wanted to help. I wanted to take one home and give it a real home.

I begged my dad over and over for a dog. We had a house with ten rooms and a backyard. But all he saw was a chance to lecture me about responsibility.

"Who's going to walk it when you're in school? Or keep it company, or take it to the vet when it gets sick? Your mom and I work."

The love part got lost somewhere in his rant. What did I end up with? A stuffed one from Toys "R" Us. Seriously. It was worse than nothing.

It's still bright out, but there's a breeze now. Entropy. That was a vocab word when I had English. It has to do with randomness, something like that, so it seems to fit now. What's illogical sounds more logical when there's an actual word to nail it down.

Entropy also sums up my random life and how I'm powerless to change it. What if I hadn't met Briggs? What if I hadn't been thrown out of school? What would the rest of my life look like? Now I was sidelined, permanently. No cheering for me, ever again. Nothing I did would make a difference. I stick my head out the window just to get air, even though it's roasting out.

The only thing you can do is change how you feel about things so they don't affect you in the same way. Not my words. Dr. Carter, the shrink my dad wasted $200 an hour on twice a week to try to reprogram my head when I got out, so I'd go back to semi-fucked from totally fucked. Talk therapy, endless talk therapy.

Too bad it didn't work.

Reprogram my feelings about Briggs and football? Not quite. The insanity of everything that happened still makes my head spin. It started in LA when I went to tryouts on a whim after school one day when I had nothing else going.

I stare out at the military trucks. Guys, just like me, standing around, looking lost.

I hadn't played football before, unless you counted the schoolyard with my dad and some friends. I was into skateboarding, swimming, snowboarding, high-speed stuff, defying the odds, making fast decisions. But I was open to something new. Maybe it was all about a secret wish to split my head open. Or more likely nail the cheerleaders. Who knows?

Without much effort I became their MVP. I remember the write-up: *At spring practice six major college coaches came from different parts of the country to watch Daughtry play.*

They talked about scholarships, cars, apartments, and the big leagues. They laughed about parties and girls. It felt unreal. My strength, the stunning pinpoint spirals I threw to my receivers. There was one word everyone kept using: potential.

They saw something in me that they didn't see in other guys.

They were actually serious.

When we moved from LA to Houston, I thought it would die down. I remember talking to my friend Adam online.

"Looking forward to anonymity. Need time to just screw up, party, whatever." I thought maybe I'd finally take more time and study acting. If there was anything that was the opposite of football for me, it was acting, and the world of living inside other people's heads. My mom was an actress before she got married, and she always encouraged me to read plays and go out for drama.

But the high school coaches around the country have some kind of old-boy network, and before I knew it Briggs had my number. I thought about turning him down, but my dad said I was crazy. Then he dangled an incentive in front of me.

"Go out for football, and I'll buy you a Harley."

I didn't think I'd heard right. "You kidding me?"

"I'm dead serious."

So I said screw it and spoke to Briggs.

That was my biggest mistake.

CHAPTER 5

15 HOURS TO LANDFALL

JILLIAN

I wake up in a sweat. I must have nodded off. The trucks, they're still there, stuck, stranded, like us. It's been less than an hour if my watch hasn't stopped. I stare out the window.

"We hardly moved in an hour?" It just comes out.

"Welcome to your highway burial plot," River says.

"Don't say that!" Why is he like that?

"Hey!" Harlan says, tapping the inside of his wrist on the steering wheel repeatedly. "This mission was badly planned. That's the problem. That is exactly the problem."

He's trapped too. Why didn't I shut up?

"The mayor screwed up. If they had evacuated us neighborhood by neighborhood, this never would have happened," Harlan says. "It would have been organized, traffic would have flowed. We wouldn't be sitting…"

"Things got worse so fast it—" I say.

"No excuse," he says. "You have drills, you prepare, and you don't let yourself be caught short."

"News flash, the world isn't perfect," River says, a muscle in his jaw pulsing.

I had thought he was lost in his music.

I stare at the soldiers on the side of the road, leaning against the trucks smoking, eyes darting back and forth. Some of them look my age.

"What are they there for?" I can't help myself.

"Water, rations, emergency care, it's not clear," Harlan says.

If we get caught in it, out here in the open? My heart starts to misfire. There's no way they can have enough supplies for everyone. Is it all for show? Like the government's trying to do something or look good? What would my mom say? I start to call her and then stop. What difference will it make? Anyway, she's busy. Too busy to talk to me now.

Out of nowhere I think of my dad, wherever he is in the world. Is he watching TV now like the rest of the country probably is? Does he think about all of us and realize where we are? He has to know that we're at the center of this. Does he feel guilty? Indifferent? Or is he in total denial? And what if he were here? What if I still had a dad? Would he be with me, or would he be out covering the story too, leaving me exactly where I am now, on my own to fend for myself?

I hate myself for still thinking of him. He doesn't even deserve that, but I can't stop. I don't deny I share his DNA. You can't pretend that doesn't exist. But the sad part is that, after all this time, I can't get beyond the pain.

I used to think it was my fault and him leaving was my punishment. I didn't listen. I was always starting fights with Ethan, with him, even with my mom, because I always wanted my own way. If I behaved better and never fought, maybe my dad would have stayed. I asked Ethan once what he thought.

"Do you think he left because of all the fights? Was it my fault?"

"Right," he said, looking at me like I was crazy. He took the book he was reading and threw it hard across the room. Then he walked out, slamming the door.

All around us, people are getting out of their cars. They're all feeling trapped too. We're together in this, we're all stuck on the highway, but really we're all feeling more alone than ever. Everyone trying not to think about the real issues. Like whether we'll survive. Whether we'll have homes to go back to if we do. Whether life will ever be the same again.

In the meantime, everyone is acting cool. People stand up and eat sandwiches, drain soda cans, change diapers on backseats, or do jobs to keep busy like pouring melted ice from their coolers, cleaning windshields, or shaking out floor mats, pretending they're being productive and moving forward with their lives. But it's all pretend, like I used to say when I was little.

My world creeps to a halt. The universe is a giant still life with touches of indistinct movement around the perimeter. The earth has stopped rotating. I am an alien watching a movie about terrestrials trying to exit the planet in the face of a giant meteorite.

Yes, I am going batshit crazy. The blistering heat is frying my brain.

Harlan stops the car. I get out and talk to the guy in the next car because it means doing something rather than nothing. "Do you have any idea what the holdup is?"

"I don't know," he says. "Maybe just too many people." That doesn't exactly help.

I go up to the car in front of him. "Have you heard anything about what's tying everything up?"

"I heard that a tractor-trailer truck broke down a mile up," he says. "But I doubt that's the problem." He shrugs. "Could just be volume."

So much for fact-finding. I get back inside.

River groans. "Why are you bothering?"

"There has to be some reason for this. It doesn't make sense."

"Make sense? What makes sense?"

I reach for my diary.

The world is divided into two kinds of people—those who are insecure and live twisted up in their fantasies, and everyone else. No doubt where I belong, watching everyone else from a safe distance in my head.

And River? He's a ticking bomb.

Traffic ahead of us moves suddenly. We shift from failure to success and edge forward. Doors slam all around us as people get back into their cars, fists of triumph in the air.

The soldiers crush out their cigarettes and disappear into the fronts and backs of the trucks. Wheels start to turn. I look at the dark canvas covers. What's shrouded beneath them?

With no explanation, traffic stays in motion. The air pressure seems to lighten as the outside streams past the windows. We're all silent, afraid to jinx it. Harlan presses buttons and the windows rise.

"OK," he says, his expression relaxing.

The AC kicks in, drying my face, the chilled air as welcome as rainbow ices on a summer afternoon. *Yes!* I want to yell out. Chalk one up for us against Mother Nature.

Success, I text Kelly. Moving finally!

Us 2. Yay!

Race u 2 Austin.

It will be fun to be with my mom's friend Linda again. She was a book reviewer before she switched to teaching. She has four Siamese cats and a pug named Waldo. Wherever you sit, the whole group wanders over and snuggles with you. At this rate, we should be there in two and a half hours.

I look at the sky for confirmation that my prayers have been answered, only it's as gray as a concrete gravestone, like the heavens don't give a crap about sending out uplifting messages.

River stretches, momentarily locking his arms around the headrest behind him. I can't not notice his biceps and the swell of his shoulders. I exhale. It comes out louder than I intended.

I thought those feelings were part of the past. Whatever. It doesn't matter. He couldn't care less. He presses his head against the seat. I'm off his radar screen, an extra piece of baggage taking up space in the backseat, Miss Ho-Hum Next-Door Neighbor, a nonentity of epic proportions.

I stare at the hands on my watch, fixating on the second hand. One minute. Two. Three. It seems to be in slow motion. I glance at the odometer. When I look again, we've gone just over two more miles. How is that possible? We slow to a crawl and stop—again.

There's nothing up ahead to explain this, downshifting from success to failure. Five minutes. Ten. Harlan kills the AC. He lowers the windows, and the toxic heat flows in. I stare at his watch, the sun bouncing off the gold, dancing like a tiny Tinkerbell on the perimeter.

Text from Kelly: Now?

Stuck again. Can't believe.

Wanna go home! she says. WHAAA.

There's a little boy in the car in the next lane. He leans out his open car door and throws up. His mom jumps out of the passenger seat and puts her hands on his shoulders, holding him. He heaves again and again and finally crouches down at the side of the hot car, crying. She tries to comfort him, but it doesn't help. River watches, wiping his forehead with the back of his hand, gnawing at the corner of his thumb.

Stop before you start bleeding, I want to say. But I don't say anything. The sun shines faintly and then fades like it's on life support before retreating behind a veil of clouds.

No, please!

River raises his sunglasses and stares up at the sky. "Twenty-four to forty-eight hours before it hits?" he says, almost to himself.

I turn to the other window. "Omigod!"

A crazy face, just outside my window, staring in at me. He's got a long gray beard and one eye is entirely milk white.

"A great evil is about to befall you, sinners!" He yells at me. "An evil greater than the Holocaust. You are about to pay for your ways— for your immorality. God is watching us and hearing our lies and we— will—pay."

"Move on," Harlan yells, starting the engine and closing the windows. But we're stuck.

The man stands there and stares through the window. At me. And then at River. I want to look away from his face—his awful, scab-covered face—but I can't.

RIVER

I watch the sick dude until he limps away to another car with his rant. Do I laugh or cry? We all sit in silence, freaked out. *Thanks, man*, I want to say, *but actually I'm more likely to die of boredom before the world ends*.

Two guys on the road watch the sick guy and laugh. Then they start tossing a football back and forth over his head, which makes as much sense as anything. Back and forth, back and forth. I watch them, hypnotized by the ball.

Part of me doesn't give a shit anymore. I'm dead to the game.

Another part of me wants to run out of the car and grab it away from them, throwing it as far as I can until it smashes down hard and gets buried deep in the ground, an all-encompassing rage burning through me for the game and what it does to you and everyone who's part of it.

My first day Briggs summoned me to see him. I went into his office at three o'clock, but he was out. There was a blackboard with nothing on it except his name in chalk letters, a foot high: COACH BRIGGS.

But what caught my eye was the birdcage on the stand in the corner. A canary? I walked over to him and whistled. He stared back at me without moving his coal-black eyes. I figured Briggs probably forgot about the appointment. I turned, ready to leave, when a booming voice came from the corridor: "River Daughtry."

I spun around, almost erupting in nervous laughter. He reminded me of a priest trying to impress a new choirboy with his godliness. He walked to the front of the room. Tall—six five maybe—with the bulk of a wrestler, jeans held up by a leather belt with a buckle as wide as a rearview mirror.

I waited, my name hanging in the air between us. I felt uneasy, not sure why.

"Sit," he said.

He stared at me from the other side of the desk, as though by peering into my head my life would open up to him. I looked back at him directly, not caring if he took the stare down like a dog that thinks it's being challenged.

"Sir."

"Welcome," he said finally. "We're glad to have you here. We'll send you for a physical—I have no doubt you'll pass it—then you can join the team. Coach Benson was very sorry to lose you." He grabbed the football on his desk like a kid needing a security blanket, touching it as if he were comforted by the feel of the grain. He held it like he earned it. I looked at it and then back at his face, pock-marked like thirty years earlier acne had hit him hard.

"Coach Benson was a great—"

"—His loss is our gain," he said, drowning me out. I sat in silence after that while he spouted off about the team and how I could get them to first place because I had "the stuff."

The stuff?

"You know what the three D's are?"

"No, sir," I said. Sir. That's how guys actually spoke here.

"Diligence, devotion, and dedication,'" he said, dead serious. "Your team is your family. You live with us, you breathe with us, you practice with us, and you give us your all. I demand one hundred percent of you." He stared at me with a paralyzing look, and I stared back. I figured he had to be totally out of his mind.

So I made the team.

And down the line came Lexie Blake. I had no idea what I was getting myself into with her.

CHAPTER 6

JILLIAN

River can't sit still. He shifts in his seat every which way, eyes fixed on two guys tossing a football, a muscle in his jaw twitching.

I keep replaying the past.

Once you met River, you couldn't not think about him. It was like he had you under his spell, which sounds cheesy and ridiculous, only it wasn't. It was true. The mop of dirty blond curls against the sharp planes of his tanned face, the disarming stare, his lean strength. I remember talking to Sari and Kelly about how hard the team worked out to stay in shape.

"Imagine running six miles and then showering before an eight o'clock class, and then after class going to practice for three hours," Sari said.

"If things are going well," Kelly added. "The other day Briggs made Ryan run another five after practice."

"They call those 'suicide runs,'" Sari said.

That didn't leave much time for studying or a life. But River must have kept his grades up because you had to, to stay on the team.

The poster on Briggs's office door summed it up best. Beneath his picture it said: "I hate losing more than I love winning."

Everyone thought it was funny.

RIVER

My dad is losing it now. The control freak can't stand feeling helpless.

"It's got to start moving," he says, surfing for traffic updates or anything to explain why in five hours we could have walked farther. Finally, we hear something. A few miles up, there's an intersection with traffic lights. The number of cars alone is slowing things to a crawl.

"Can't they just turn off the lights and let traffic pass through?" Jillian asks.

"That would make too much sense," my dad says.

I drop half a pill down my throat. He sees it and turns back to the road clenching his jaw. Some days I think about downing the whole goddamn bottle. At least the craziness would go away. Forever.

Jillian's texting again. Must be killing her dick boyfriend to know she's in the car with the big, bad wolf. That's something to smile about anyway.

CHAPTER 7

14 HOURS TO LANDFALL

JILLIAN

Text from Aidan. How's it going?

Boring. U?

Better if you were here. Xo.

Aidan opens doors for me, takes me to dinner and the movies, and even does sweet things like buy me ladybug earrings for my birthday and perfume from Victoria's Secret.

"It's sweet, and so are you," said his card to me on my birthday. Kind of Hallmark-y, but cute.

And it was cool to go to the basketball games and sit in a reserved front-row seat to watch him play, seeing him glance out at me as if he were playing for me alone. Sometimes he'd wink at me before a free throw, as if to say, "Watch me ace this," and then look back at me and smile after he made the basket.

What I don't tell anyone is that when we kiss and he says, "I love you," I don't always say it back.

"Don't you love Aidan?" Kelly once asked me.

"I totally like him. If you love someone at first sight, it usually goes downhill from there." I'd read that somewhere. It sounded reasonable.

Kelly rolled her eyes. "Who came up with that theory?"

Right or wrong, I was the only one of my friends who hadn't seriously hooked up with anyone. So when Aidan came along, he seemed perfect. He liked me, he wanted to be with me, and he had a brain—aside from math, that is—and a great body. What more could I want?

Most of the girls and all the gay guys in school have crushed on Aidan, but he doesn't seem to be aware of it, or he pretends he isn't. I'm the only one he's interested in.

When he found out my mom was staying in Houston to cover the storm, but I was leaving with River and Harlan, he freaked.

"River?"

"And his dad."

Aidan hates River, despises even hearing his name ever since the picnic—almost six months ago. If I just mention him in passing, Aidan's face will turn cold.

"Don't go with them...come with us," he said, insistently. "We have an Expedition, there's so much room."

"You're acting like I'm running away with him. His dad is driving. They'll be dropping me off. I'll be fine."

"It doesn't bother you?"

"What?"

"Being with River," he said, like I was a moron.

"You're making it into this whole big thing. I'll be in the backseat by myself, texting you and playing games on my phone."

46

"He's got this dark history," he said. "You don't know the things they say about him and why he was thrown out...they—"

"—If my mom's not worried, why are you?"

"Jillian..." his voice trailed off and he went silent the way he always does when he gets mad.

• • •

I sit in the backseat—sweat dripping down my face, watching people outside eating sandwiches out of a picnic basket—and I replay that night. Last April, less than six months ago. The school's annual full-moon picnic.

After the drama club put on the play, we swarmed the picnic tables like locusts, eating the six-foot hero sandwiches and then playing Frisbee. The Frisbee got tossed out into the field, and I went searching for it in the dark. Only River got there before me. He found me hunting for it and wouldn't give it back until I kissed him. That was the crazy tradition—at the full-moon picnic, everyone had to kiss someone.

"Initiate me," he said with his flirty smile.

I started to object, not sure how to explain, and then decided that was silly. He'd just give me a quick kiss on the cheek. Why make a big deal of it?

But River saw it differently.

He eased toward me, his face so close I could feel the heat of his skin. I thought he'd kiss me right away, but he didn't, not at first. He took his thumb and rubbed it across my bottom lip, back and forth, back and forth, and then slowly and softly, his lips met mine. Out of nowhere the heat flared up between us. An attraction that I didn't know existed left me nearly powerless. Chemistry. I'd heard the word a thousand times before, but until then, I'd never understood what it meant.

River knew how to kiss, really kiss. Not like Aidan. Not like anyone I had ever kissed before. For just a few seconds, I let myself kiss him back, meeting his soft, slow, intoxicating rhythm. Neither of us wanted to stop, but then I did. I told him I had a boyfriend.

And out of nowhere, Aidan's face appeared—and everything exploded.

• • •

The thrum of a text jars me from my thoughts.

Kelly. How's it going?

Standing still. You?

Stuck in sucky traffic. Stopping next gas station. How's R?

Not talking to me much. I bite at my lip.

Better.

River zones when he's not making snarky comments. Part of me just wants someone to talk to, to connect with to pass the time, but I'm not about to start a lame conversation. Do you miss football? How's your job at Whole Foods? You into quinoa now?

He's closed off. Not that it matters. After today, who knew if we'd even be alive. If only my mom were here, or Kelly or Sari. We'd be singing with our music, talking about kids in our grade, or playing dumb games instead of sitting in stony silence. We should all be mocking Danielle, showing her what we think of her. I should have gone with Aidan.

I text, **Wish I were with you.**

Me too. Luv you.

"Anyone want snacks or water?" Harlan reaches into a food bag and takes out a gallon-size Ziploc bag of granola bars.

"Thanks, I'm good," I say.

He unwraps one and bites into it, filling the air with a gross peanut smell.

"I feel sick," River says, staring out the window.

"Open the door, get some air," Harlan says. "It's not like we're going anywhere."

River doesn't move.

I open the window far enough to slide my arm out and then draw it back, running my fingers over my skin. Sweat? Moisture in the air? Or my imagination? But it isn't. The windshield is clouding over with a misting of rain.

This so sucks, I text Sari.

My blood is standing still, she says. So packed in, impossible to move.

"The jerk meteorologists are wrong as usual," River says, punching the sunroof. A moment later he opens his seat belt and reaches up to turn a knob that slides opens the sunroof.

What is he doing?

RIVER

I can't sit in this goddamn car anymore and wait to die. I feel like my hands are tied behind me in a straitjacket and I can't move. I flash back to the center and want to heave. I thought those things were used centuries ago, that even hellholes like the one I was in had abandoned them. I was wrong.

I watch my dad. He sits there without moving, his face showing nothing. I wonder sometimes if he has feelings anymore or whether everything inside him has dried up and all that's left is a hard shell— the focused badass marine who has a job to do and does it without questioning anything or listening to anybody else.

Retreat, hell!

Ready for all, yielding to none.

He's so brainwashed by their mottos he closes himself off to the truth.

I stare around me at the scene, and it's like watching a horror movie about life on earth about to end. I want to get away from this goddamn car and these people. I want to run. It's the only way I feel alive. It's the only way I know I still have a beating heart inside me. Running stops the pain. It stops the panic. It stops the memories. Christ, I need to get out of this car. *Now!* I slam my fist into the roof and enjoy the pain.

JILLIAN

"Danielle," River yells out, making a megaphone with his hands as he stands up on the seat, his head outside the car. "You stupid bitch."

"River," his dad says, in a low, controlled voice, "get back inside."

"You bitch," River yells even louder. "B-i-t-c-h. B-i-t-c-h, b-i-t-c-h, b-i-t-c-h, b-i-t-c-h. Eight hours away, huh? You're right above our heads, aren't you?"

He's yelling at the top of his lungs, like he's trying to connect with a sound system in heaven that will carry him on its frequency so he has a direct line to Danielle.

"B-i-t-c-h, b-i-t-c-h, b-i-t-c-h," he goes on, probably ripping his vocal cords out.

Fury, rage, all pouring out of him. Do I laugh or cry? He starts pounding, pounding, pounding his fists on the roof of the car.

BOOM, BOOM, BOOM BOOM BOOM.

"Stupid fucking gas guzzler, traffic victim," he yells. "I could have gone to Austin and back on my bike by now." He pounds and keeps pounding.

"River!" Harlan yells again. "You're going to smash the goddamned roof in."

People in the cars around us are staring now, convinced they're watching an insane person. But then their faces start to change, and they're laughing with him because he's giving voice to what everyone is thinking and feeling. They're all as angry and frustrated as he is, ready to shriek their heads off too because of how this freakish storm has disrupted their lives, not knowing what, if anything, they'll have when they return, and it scares the hell out of them.

Only they're also probably thinking why bother, what good would it do? They're hot, thirsty, and tired enough, so let him be the show.

River doesn't have to worry about getting busted for disturbing the peace. The cops couldn't get to him if they tried.

Harlan stares out his side window, a vein in his jaw throbbing.

"Danielle," River yells out again, just when I thought he would stop. "Are you going to kill us all, huh? Drown us, or what? Tell me, I want to hear the plan. Are you going to blow our heads off, or drown us after you destroy our lives and everything around us while we're jailed in our cars trying to escape you? You're a sadistic bitch, Danielle."

He goes on like that.

"You lowlife bbbbbbbbiiiiiiiiiiiitttttttttcccccccch."

"River," Harlan says in a low, measured voice. River still ignores him, and Harlan's face reddens. "River!" he says, punching the steering wheel.

When is he going to stop? Is he completely out of his mind? I grab my water. A tiny sip and then I press my head into the back of the seat. An ink-blot of sweat darkens River's red T-shirt at the small of his back, like some mutant butterfly from a Rorschach test. When he lifts his arms, I see a swath of skin with a tattoo across the small of his back. It reads: *Never. Give. In.*

Standing and yelling his head off eventually wears him out. He reaches for water and downs half a bottle. I focus on something in one of his back pockets as he ducks back down into his seat.

A knife.

Take only what's essential.

River turns to his dad. "We're never going to make it to Austin," he says in a whisper, like someone bipolar who has slid back to calm.

"What are you talking about?"

He wipes his sweating face with the back of his hand. "Open your eyes, look at the sky."

Harlan looks up and then back at River. He doesn't answer.

RIVER

I don't want to start this, but I'm out of options. I turn to face her for the first time since we left. Our eyes lock. Her face is flushed, hot, sweat dots the curve of her full upper lip. She looks away first.

"We have to get inside somewhere."

She looks back to me, narrowing her eyes. "What do you mean?"

"If we stay in this car we're dead; we'll be caught in the middle of it."

"You don't know that for sure."

"No? Look at the sky. We might have a few hours, maybe less. Traffic isn't moving, more and more cars are going to get on the highway as the weather gets worse. You don't have to be Einstein to know if we stay here we'll be buried. This is a death trap."

My dad scratches the back of his head. "River, it's not going to hit so soon. We'll move. We'll get to Austin, OK? Stop freaking out."

"Stop freaking out?" I turn to him, furious. "Reality check. You're the one who should be freaking out." His jaw tightens.

Jillian's face darkens as the truth hits her. My dad's impassive stare says I'm right, only he can't admit it, he won't, because he doesn't know what to do, and he's in charge here, or he thinks he should be.

But since when does being older make you right? *Sorry, dude, you're blowing this mission. Your troops are dead in the water if they follow you.*

Jillian looks at the sky. Is her psycho neighbor right or not? Should she trust me? Tough call. I doubt I'd trust me.

I wish my grandmother were here. When bad weather was coming, she used to say, "I feel it in my bones." She was always right, like she had a direct line to the universe. It blew me away. What would my dad say to her now if she were here and could predict how much time we had? Knowing him, he'd blow her off.

The sky's already changing, the wind building.

"We'll get off at the next exit, gas up, and take stock," my dad says, because it sounds like a plan. "We don't have many options. It's either stay on the road which might open up, or get out and get stuck in what, some overcrowded gas station or 7-Eleven without our things?" He looks around and shakes his head. "We're in the middle of nowhere. No hotels. What's here—fast food joints, a body shop? What would we do, sleep in the car? Under an overpass? My vote is to keep going unless we hear different."

Sure. Exactly what he would say.

"Life or death without a survival guide," I whisper. Jillian looks at me and opens her mouth to speak, but no words come out.

"My vote is go back to Houston," I say. "We've gone less than fifteen miles. Turn around and floor it and we'll be back in ten minutes. It's a big city. There are brick buildings, places to hide. Everything can't be closed."

"We're not going back," my dad says. "They told us to evacuate. You're suggesting we drive back into the center of the storm? The hotels are all closed. What would we do, break in somewhere?"

"I'm suggesting we think for ourselves," I insist. "We could find a place to hole up. Something solid. The roads are totally open going back." I see the look on his face. He never listens, never cares what I think.

"Exactly where would we go?"

"A shelter or something. I'll find a place. It beats sitting in the middle of a jam-packed highway like a target."

"Or something?" he repeats, like I'm crazy. "The traffic will pick up; it'll start to move. At least we're going in the right direction."

I stare at my dad, my fists tightening. "Just look at what's ahead of you on the highway. You're a prisoner. You don't have a chance. Why is it so hard to admit you're wrong?"

CHAPTER 8

JILLIAN

River pops pills, throws knives, and yells at the sky. I eat myself up inside with fear because time is running out. Which one of us is crazy? Which one is sane? Which one of us knows the right thing to do?

Monster storm. Monster storm. I keep replaying the nightmare. Why did I have it? What did it mean—assuming dreams give you insights and aren't just a jumble of your fears, the wreckage left behind from the storms in different chapters of your life.

I go back to the day my dad left. I couldn't breathe as I stared at him through my bedroom window and watched him get into the car and drive away, leaving us to get along on our own.

But why did I dream it? Was it a warning about what was to come? Would I be orphaned again, this time by Danielle? Would I keep losing my way and be powerless to do anything about it?

It wouldn't be the first time someone dreamed what was later going to come true. It wouldn't be the first time the future would have the power to affect the past, as crazy as that sounded. I ended up telling Kelly.

"It's because you're not from here and this is new to you," she said. "We're used to tornados and hurricanes and—" She waved it away. "We take it in stride because we get hit with crazy weather all the time, so we just ride it out."

"Ride it out?"

"Shit happens here," she said, "get used to it." She laughed. "What doesn't kill you, makes you stronger."

Kelly was probably right. I tried to distract myself by keeping busy. As soon as I got home from school, I went swimming. If I was worn out, I'd crash when my head hit the pillow. Exhaustion would drive the nightmare away.

Our pool is nothing fancy, just a big rectangle, half of it surrounded with plants with blue flowers that are bigger than snow cones. In the summer it's my oasis of coolness and calm. While I was doing laps, I remembered something that happened before River disappeared from school. It was just a few months after he moved in next door. It was November, but it was still warm enough to swim.

I wanted to work at the town pool for the summer instead of interning and being stuck inside an office all day, so I was determined to pass the lifeguard test. There were four parts to it. The first was to swim two hundred yards in four minutes or less. I measured off the distance, basically two-and-a-half laps in our pool. I was in the zone. In my fantasy I was an Olympic contender, training for the competition. I was so lost in my daydreams that I didn't realize anyone else was around. Then I looked up.

It was like seeing a mirage, ripples of heat distorting my vision. River was standing at the edge of the pool watching me, the late afternoon sun bathing him in a golden light. There was something surreal about seeing

56

him still as a statue, unruly curls framing his face, red board shorts slung low on his hips.

"You scared me!" I tried to catch my breath, pushing the wet hair away from my eyes. I hoisted myself up and sat on the side of the pool, trying to catch my breath. "I didn't see you come in."

"Sorry, I called you, but I guess you didn't hear me."

He dropped down next to me, put his feet in the water. We gazed at each other, neither of us saying anything, the silence growing strained, even though it couldn't have been more than a few seconds. A dragonfly swooped down, skimming its iridescent blue-green wings along the surface of the water, before rising up and perching itself on River's shoulder, its wings fluttering, the insect equivalent of a preening peacock.

Even bugs are drawn to him. I almost laughed.

His lips curled up into a smile. He blew at it softly, and the dragonfly lifted off. I followed its flight and then glanced back at River.

"In half an hour, they can devour an amount of food equal to their entire body weight."

"I don't remember learning that in bio," he said, smirking. "I must have been out sick that day."

"No, that came from the inside of a Snapple lid."

"I have a lot in common with dragonflies then," he said, "I'm always starved too."

Our eyes met and everything inside me seized up. I turned away, reaching for the towel on the lounge chair behind me, wrapping it tightly around my shoulders.

Without a word, River leaned toward me and lifted a strand of wet hair off my cheek, tucking it behind my ear, his knuckles grazing my face. He lifted a second strand on the other side with the same light stroke of his fingers, slipping it behind the other ear.

It wasn't anything, the lightest touch. It meant nothing. But the sensation shot through me, setting off painful stings of longing, which was crazy and confusing. I swallowed hard and finally looked away. I had a boyfriend, this was wrong. River probably came on to girls all the time, to see who and what he could get. Guys like him did that. Why not?

"So," I said abruptly, "why did you—"

"You're not getting enough air on the intake," he said, turning serious.

"What?"

"When you swim. You're not getting enough air when you inhale because you're not getting enough out at the exhale."

"You can see that?"

"I used to swim competitively, and we videotaped ourselves so we could study our form and see what we were doing wrong."

"Oh…well…thanks. I'll try to exhale harder. Next time."

"Try it now," he said, motioning for me to get back into the pool. "I'll watch you."

I hesitated.

"Go on," he said, motioning to the water.

I got back in and he followed me in. He swam alongside me, watching intently as I went from one end of the pool to the other, working at breathing out harder and then deliberately taking in more air. Finally I stopped and looked up at him questioningly.

"Better," he said. "How does it feel?"

I shrugged. "I'm not sure. How's it supposed to feel?"

"Keep going. You'll know."

Why did everything he said sound like…

I kept swimming and so did he, keeping pace with me. He seemed to really care that I got it right. When I stopped he held his hand up for a high five.

"You got it," he said, his hand hitting mine. "You'll see, you'll swim stronger now."

"I'm taking the lifeguard test for a job at the pool," I said, climbing out of the water. Why did I tell him? He didn't ask.

"Cool," he said, following me out. "Which pool?"

"West U."

"Wow," he said. "I just applied for that too. What a coincidence."

"Really?"

"Yeah, I definitely want that job."

"Oh." Why was I wasting my time preparing? I didn't stand a chance.

He looked at me straight-faced for a moment and then laughed. "I'm kidding."

I could feel my face turning pink. So I was a total dork.

"River one, Jillian nothing," I said, writing the score in the air with my finger.

"Not nothing," he whispered, his eyes holding mine. "Definitely not nothing."

He stepped toward me. The air between us was charged. It was late afternoon. The sun was low in the sky, warming my back. My mom was out. So was Ethan. It was just the two of us, our bodies inches apart.

And he was still staring.

I swallowed, trying to ignore the steady stream of water droplets trickling down my shoulders and back, slipping inside my suit.

He lowered his gaze to my lips.

I needed air.

"So," I blurted out, trying to draw a breath. "Was that why you came over...because of how I swim? Or just to goof on me?"

He grinned, socking his head. "Hell no, I nearly forgot. Our refrigerator died and my dad wanted to know if we could use your freezer until tomorrow when the new fridge comes. If you have room. And you don't mind if—"

"—It's fine."

"Cool." He laughed. "Or cold, or whatever." He headed toward the back door of his house, our backyard gate slamming behind him. A few minutes later it slammed again and he was back with a stack of frozen dinners under his arm. He looks embarrassed.

"Frozen food," he said. "It's what's for dinner."

"You really live on those?"

"Uh…yeah. We don't cook much…" A flicker of sadness passed over his face, and then it vanished.

Why hadn't I just shut up? He didn't have a mom, and his dad worked. Who was there to cook for him or worry about what he ate?

"I'm sorry, I didn't mean…"

"No worries."

"I just meant I know the coach gets on your case about eating right, so—"

"Right," he said, nodding robotically.

"You're almost in first place, so I guess he doesn't want to…"

He looked off, waiting impatiently.

"River?"

"What?" he said, turning back to me.

"You can use the pool anytime you want. We're hardly ever out here."

"Thanks," he said, the smile returning. "I'll take you up on that."

The following week at about ten at night I was upstairs on the phone. Absentmindedly, I walked to the window. The house lights cast enough of a glow for me to see him swimming from one end of the pool to the other, over and over.

I started counting to see how many laps he'd do, but he kept going back and forth, back and forth, in a regular rhythm and I lost count, eventually turning away. I thought about going outside and bringing him cookies and lemonade. Maybe he was thirsty. Or wouldn't have minded taking a break. But I didn't want to bother him, or break into his fantasies, whatever they were.

• • •

The honking of horns draws me out of my thoughts. River and his dad ignore each other, their barriers up even though they sit nearly shoulder to shoulder in the front seat. The stony silence is pushing me to take sides. There's no middle ground. Stay in the car? Come up with another plan? I look at my watch. I'm on a game show with only seconds left before I need to answer—that's how it feels.

The sky is changing color, everything deepening to a mix of silvery grays with shots of white light, but the shift is so subtle I feel I need to take pictures, to prove it to myself, so I know I'm not imagining it. We may be trapped in place, unable to move, but nothing's holding Danielle back. She's slowly building strength, getting ready to stage her life-altering performance.

So typical of us women. Hazardous, wildly unpredictable! At least that's what male meteorologists used to think—that's why they used only female names for hurricanes. I wrote that in my hurricane article for the school paper. Then, hello, that sexist practice got scrapped in 1978 when more women entered the field and the hurricanes were given male names too.

It takes nearly half an hour for us to creep to the next exit. I watch the sky, trying to scope out Danielle like she's a girl who's a threat, someone you can't turn your back on. I feel like screaming at her too. She is a bitch. This is all her fault.

Finally Harlan pulls into a gas station and gets into a long line of cars waiting for a pump. River goes to buy a drink. I head for the bathroom line that snakes along the side of the building. One bathroom, unisex.

As I stand there, two guys a little older than me get in line behind me. "Jenna?" one of them says, almost in my ear. I shake my head.

"You sure?" he says, laughing. "You're like her twin."

No, I'm not sure. I don't know who I am.

"Where you from?" he says.

I ignore him.

"What, you don't want to talk?"

I still ignore him.

"You speak English?" he says, and then laughs.

"Shut up, Mike," his friend says.

"What did I do? She's hot, OK? I'm into redheads. Anyway, if we're all gonna die here, might as well enjoy ourselves before we go."

At that point I want to disappear, but that's not happening and I need the bathroom and the line is long and where is River, or Harlan, or anybody?

Fingers slide through the back of my hair.

"Don't!" It comes out louder than I intended. Everyone in line is staring at me now, and my face is turning crimson. I look around and then spot River watching from a distance. He walks over and steps between me and the guys.

"You have a problem?"

The first one laughs. "We don't have a problem."

"Good," River says, still staring at them, the closed knife visible in his hand. He clicks open the blade and slides it very lightly against the palm of his right hand, again and again as if he's testing the sharpness.

"Let's go," one of them says. "Line's too long. We can pee behind the trees, that's why God invented them." The other one shrugs and finally they amble away.

I look at River. "Thanks."

He shakes his head and closes the knife. He slides out the pill bottle, looks at it, and puts it back in his pocket.

"What are those?"

"Pills."

"Thanks, I couldn't tell."

But I see the label. Ativan. They're addictive, I know that. So he's a pill junkie, great, but does that make him wrong about the storm? He opens the knife and snaps it shut. Click. Snap. Click. Snap. Again and again, rhythmically, before sliding the blade slowly over the inside of his palm again. Snap.

Ahead of us in line a girl with dark curls and blue eyes who looks six or seven is watching him, her eyes fixed on the knife. She leans into her mom.

"I'm not going back to the car," he says, turning to me.

I don't answer.

"You coming with me?"

I suck in a deep breath and shake my head. "No." My default answer in life. Like a two-year-old.

"Mistake." He narrows his eyes. "Why not?"

"I think it's safer to be in a car than out on the road. What if the wind picks up or the rain gets heavy? What are you going to do on foot?"

"There are safer places than a goddamned car."

"Like?"

Before he can answer, Harlan comes back. "So?"

River looks at his dad like he's a complete idiot. "I'm not going with you."

"River..."

"You're dead if you stay in the car. How can you not see that?"

"And on foot? Where are you going to go? Where are you going to find food or water? You going to loot a supermarket? And then what, you get busted again, sent back?"

River seems to recoil.

"I know the traffic is insane," Harlan says, slightly softening his tone, "but it'll pick up. We have time, Austin's not that far."

River snorts. "In this traffic? I'll give it one hour. If we don't start moving by then, I'm gone."

He gives up on the bathroom line and goes behind a bush. But not me. I wait my turn and finally go, sliding the metal bolt to lock the door. The seat is wet, gross. It smells horrible in this dark, airless space. I rest my head in my hands, massaging my throbbing scalp, willing the right answer to come to me. I press my fingers against my eyes, creating a black field as though I'm in outer space.

"C'mon, let's go," someone yells from outside, rattling the doorknob.

"OK!" No soap, no toilet paper, no towels, and the dryer doesn't work. I find a used tissue in my pocket. I rinse my hands and throw cold water on my face before heading out and wedging myself back into the car. Harlan starts the engine.

And I start praying.

13 HOURS TO LANDFALL

RIVER

Text from Ryan, the only guy from school who hasn't cut me loose. The only one who had a life off the field.

Praying you're safe. Riding it out at home.

He's in deeper shit than us. They live in a trailer home, and his dad is in a wheelchair. Ryan bikes to school. If they even have a car, it's some old piece of garbage. Get to a brick building, somewhere safe, I text back. Get the hell out of your house, man. It'll blow.

My first days in school, he was one of the few guys who offered to show me around. After I joined the team, he pulled me aside and warned me about Briggs.

"Don't screw around with him," he said. "Football is his life."

Ryan knew Briggs too well. If you didn't pledge yourself to him with your life, you paid the price. And Briggs knew how to push everyone's buttons. He was a vengeful prick, and you didn't dare cross him, no matter what he did. I reach down and feel for my knife.

I do want to kill him, I wish I had. It's all his fault.

I glance at Jillian through the rearview mirror and for the briefest moment, our eyes meet. I look away.

I can't help thinking of the picnic again.

Ryan told me about that too. "They call it the full-moon picnic because there was one the first year they had it. And there's this tradition."

"What kind?" I asked, grinning.

"Like the kiss under the mistletoe, you have to kiss someone under the moonlit sky, or the imagined moonlit sky. It can be anyone. Someone you're seeing, someone you want to be seeing, or just a friend."

It sounded like something from the sixties. I expected DJs spinning vinyls. I thought of Carla, a would-be actress, my last girlfriend in LA. She would have enjoyed dressing the part.

"It starts at sundown," Ryan said, "and goes until nine thirty or ten, unless..."

"Unless what?"

"Someone's parents are away. Then it can last all night."

The high-school picnic, an innocent night of fun. It turned out to be anything but. It was more of an earthquake. First losing myself with Jillian. Then getting the crap knocked out of me in the fight. And if that wasn't enough, being stupid enough to let myself be led into a sick relationship with Lexie.

There was no full moon that night to put the blame on. The sky was dark. I should have had my eyes open. I should have seen what I was doing. But the star football player got sidelined by want and need. My head was someplace else, so I fumbled and dropped the ball. And from there everything went downhill.

CHAPTER 9

JILLIAN

Text from Aidan. How's it going?

Um…too slow!

Yeah, this sucks.

I think back to my last night with Aidan. Dinner at Tío Pepe. Then we drove around, stopping on a dark street near a playground. He leaned toward me with a serious look in his eyes.

"What if we never see each other again?" he said, running his fingers under the edge of my sleeveless blouse, sliding my bra strap down over my shoulder.

"Don't say that. We'll see each other."

He leaned over and started kissing me so hard that the seat jerked down under me. I pulled away to take a breath. "Aidan…"

"I love you," he said, pulling me toward him and then straddling me, his jeans rough against the skin of my thighs. "You know that, right?"

I kissed him back in answer, letting him open my blouse and finally reach under my skirt. He'd only done that once before. It wasn't that I wanted him to. It was just that I couldn't think of a reason to make him stop, especially the night before we'd be leaving—separately—not knowing what would happen. If I stopped him we'd break up, and I wasn't ready to do anything that required making a real decision.

I wasn't good at making decisions. I didn't have much practice. My mom made them for me. She always knew best. Supermom did everything for me and Ethan because there was no dad to turn to.

But you grow up. Or you're supposed to. You think for yourself and figure out what's right for you. I opened my eyes and stared at Aidan.

Having sex right then would say something about how we felt about each other, with everything ahead. Only my mind kept stalling out, focusing on how I was sweating with the AC off, my armpits stinging with wetness. I was almost faint.

"We should just do it," Aidan whispered in a husky voice. "Before we go."

"Did you bring something?"

"I'll be careful, I swear."

"Aidan, you know we—"

"—we said we'd do it, Jill. You know you want to—"

Instead of answering, I kissed him back, hating myself for not feeling what I was supposed to, for getting crazed by voices in my head shouting *This is a huge deal, you have to want this,* and a moment later, *It isn't. Stop being a baby and grow up!*

But no matter how hard I tried to feel something, I couldn't get beyond this anger at myself. All I could think of was the distance between us I couldn't cross. Did I resent Aidan for putting me in that position, or myself for not knowing what to do? The more we kissed, the more strung out I felt.

Then I went into a free fall, trying in just the few seconds left as he tugged at my panties and his breathing got ragged, to figure out whether I felt anything for Aidan or whether I was acting like a mindless robot.

"Aidan," my voice said, coming out pleading and unrecognizable. He was breathing faster and harder and he leaned away from me for a minute to open his belt buckle and unzip his jeans, his face glistening. I watched him as droplets of sweat ran down the sides of his face, dripping onto mine, seeing him like a stranger, trying to figure out what he meant to me. What made it worse was he wasn't seeing me at all because he was so caught up in his own need, like sex was all about him.

Just as he tugged his jeans down over his hips, his face caught fire.

"What the hell?" he said, looking up suddenly, his breathless voice filled with panic.

A brilliant, flashing light pierced the windshield, lighting us up like lovers on a movie-set with giant floods.

"Holy shit," he said, scrunching down in his seat, yanking up his jeans as I grabbed at the sides of my shirt to button it. What idiots we were not to have known. What were we thinking? After dark the cops patrolled the park. We should have watched for them. We should have thought of that. But we didn't think about anything except ourselves.

The cop who was driving got out of the car and walked toward us, his partner behind him, their headlights focused on their targets. The first cop was young, maybe twenty-five. Even though his right hand was resting back lightly on the handle of his gun, he seemed more amused than anything.

"You can't park here," he said, a smirk on his face. His partner came around to my side and stared at us through the window.

"Sorry," Aidan said, "we'll leave now."

"I could take you in...or get your names," he shook his head, "but I'm a nice guy, so consider this a warning. If I see you here again, I'll take you in." They walked back to their car and turned off their lights. It gave us the time we needed.

"Shit," Aidan said, buckling his belt. "Who the hell thought—"

"—We didn't," I said, turning away. Hot tears filled my eyes. I stared out the window so he couldn't see. Why was I crying like a baby? I buttoned my blouse and straightened my skirt, then wiped my eyes. If he noticed, he didn't say anything. He started the car and pulled away slowly. Through the rearview mirror, I saw their headlights go on. They drove away after we did.

"What do you want to do now?"

I let out the breath I didn't know I was holding. "Go home, what do you think?"

He lifted his hands off the wheel, holding them out helplessly. "So now you're mad at me?"

"I'm tired, Aidan." But I was mad. Or scared. Or something. Everything felt like it was his fault, or at least I wanted it to be.

CHAPTER 10

RIVER

The people in the car next to us are eating hamburgers. I think back to the two times that Briggs took the team out for steak dinners. It was always quid pro quo with him. You scored, you won, the beast fed you. And they weren't just dinners, they were over the top, like everything Briggs did.

We went to the most expensive restaurants in town, all of us dressed up like goons in jackets and ties, even though it was nearly a hundred degrees outside. We ordered up everything on the damn menu, starting with those towers of cold seafood, then lettuce wedges with blue cheese dressing, Caesar salads, rib eyes, filet mignons, onion rings, baked potatoes, and fries. Briggs must have spent half a year's salary on each dinner, but I doubt he cared. He probably didn't have anything else to do with his money anyway. No wife, as far as any of us knew. No anyone. He was alone. Always alone. I couldn't imagine him having friends. Who the hell would choose to hang out with him? I don't think he ever cracked a smile or laughed, unless it was in a derogatory way, to crush someone.

I remember those dinners because despite the food, I never forgot that bite by bite, I was entering into an implied bargain. The meal was a payoff for the games we played, but it was also our promise to continue to win. And if we didn't? He'd demand his pound of flesh. There was no such thing as a free meal, especially when Briggs was footing the bill.

JILLIAN

Sometimes I can still glimpse the River I used to know, before he changed 180 degrees. The one who wrote a play that he absentmindedly left on a desk in the drama room because he hoped to join the drama club, not realizing that snoopy me would pick it up and read it. I can't forget the title: *Hypocrite*.

I'm haunted by whatever happened to him. I watch his face, his expressions. There's so much anger and frustration inside him now. He's going to bolt from the car, I know it. There's no way he'll stay here.

The question is what do I do? Can I trust him? How can I know if he's right?

I text my mom.

River thinks we'll never get to Austin. Harlan thinks traffic will start moving. What to do?

Stay with Harlan, she answers, almost instantaneously. You won't get anywhere on foot. You're in a car, and you have food and water. Listen to him.

Before I can blink, my phone rings.

"What the hell are you thinking, J?"

My mom must have speed-dialed Ethan because there is no way he would have called on his own. Proof that she's freaking. I don't answer.

"Jill," he says, "what are you planning?"

"Who is this?"

"Haha," he says. "There's a hurricane coming, if you haven't heard, little sister. So as the only sane member of the family, I hope you'll listen to me and stay with Harlan instead of that head-freak son of his."

Ethan likes River. They've played guitar together, even hung out together.

"I'm touched by your concern. Where are you?"

"Near La Grange."

"La Grange?" I kick myself for not insisting on going with them. They were halfway to Austin. No doubt they'd make it.

"We stayed off 290 and took crapola side streets," Ethan says. "I guess we got lucky."

"So Mom told you to call me?"

"No..."

"Liar, liar, pants on fire."

"OK, she did, but for what it's worth, this is one of the few times I think she's right, and Jill..." There's a long pause. "I love you, little sister," he says, his voice breaking. "So just listen to me, OK, for once in your pathetic life?"

I try to answer, but the words catch in my throat. In my entire life, I don't think Ethan has ever said that. "I'll think about it."

"OK."

"And Ethan?"

"Yeah?"

"Love you too, lowlife."

CHAPTER 11

RIVER

I stare at the sky. Who's your first victim, Danielle, the pathetic little kid in the car next to us playing with his puppy? His mom? I see visions of myself when I was his age and then I try to forget them and sleep, but I'm drowning in sweat. Small favors, traffic starts moving again. Drivers get back into their seats and engines start. Windows close and the air kicks in. But I know this is bullshit. It's a tease, so we'll lower our defenses.

We cruise along at the breakneck speed of 15 miles an hour—as far as you can get from the empty roads in West Texas where you can hit 110 without getting pulled over, not that there's anything out there you want to rush to get to.

We slow to a stop after less than three miles. I study my dad's face. He has to sense me looking, but he focuses straight ahead, his expression blank. Is he thinking about my mom and what she would do if she were here?

Backseat. Jillian's texting. Does she think her friends know more than she does? Near us a couple and two kids get out of their car. They stretch and stare ahead, waving at people in a car ahead of them. The driver of the other car takes out a camera and films them. Right man, make a movie of this. Put it on YouTube. I look at my phone. Forty-five minutes since we stopped at the gas station. Fifteen more, then screw it, I'm out of here.

JILLIAN

My insides tighten as I watch River checking the time on his phone. What if he does get out and start to run? Should I go with him? Or stay? Will Harlan even let him go? What can he do to stop him?

No one expected a traffic jam like this. If my mom had, would she have let me go? She must have picked up my vibes because my phone rings.

"How are you doing?"

"We're gridlocked."

"How's Harlan doing?"

Freaking out only he can't show us that he is. "OK…I guess."

"I heard that the tie-up is close to Austin," she says. "But they're going to open up more contraflow lanes."

"What's that?"

"They're going to turn more traffic lanes that usually go into Houston into lanes going out. That should help."

"But the storm…isn't it going to hit us sooner?"

She hesitates. "Maybe." She's working on acting calm, but I know my mom.

"River wants to bail," I whisper, even though I know he can hear me. "What?"

"Hide out somewhere. He doesn't think we're going to make it to Austin."

"Hide out?" she says, her voice rising. "You're in the middle of 290."

"Not here on the highway, back in Houston."

"What's he going to do, go running back?" she says, not waiting for an answer. "When it hits there will be downed power lines, trees falling, flooding, wind gusts." I hear panic in her voice. "Jillian, you can't be outside. You have no idea what it's like to be in a hurricane. Running back on foot is crazy. Didn't Harlan tell him that?"

"But suffocating in the car is OK?" I don't know which one of us is crazier, or what makes sense or doesn't or if it makes any difference at all. This is pick-your-poison time.

It reminds me of the "would you rather" games we used to play when we had sleepovers. That seems like a lifetime ago, when Sari, Kelly, and I had our Friday night pajama parties. When we were tucked into our safe little beds, we enjoyed scaring ourselves by imagining all the horrible scenarios we might face and then asking ourselves which one was worse and how we'd choose to die.

Would you rather die in an airplane crash or a car crash?

Would you rather get chewed to death by a mountain lion or bitten by a black widow spider?

Never did I imagine that one day in the real world I'd be asking myself, *Would you rather die from a hurricane in a car on the freeway or outside running for shelter?*

River turns, x-raying my head. What does he hope to find out? I feel like the fly on the wall, listening to myself as if I'm hearing a stranger. Am I agreeing with him? I'm not sure when that happened.

"Stay with Harlan," she says in an exaggeratedly calm voice, like she's talking to an idiot. "I have to speak to New York, but call me back and give me an update."

She wants to hang up so she can talk to the office, a friend, anyone. She's out of arguments and needs to regroup. She's probably frantically checking on the traffic to see if we're doomed either way.

Harlan's eyes meet mine briefly in the mirror. He doesn't know me at all. Am I like his son? He needs an ally here. He can't think of any arguments to keep us where we are though. Even if he agreed with River, what would he do, make a U-turn and fast track it back to Houston? Ditch his car and try to make it somewhere on foot? I've never seen him running, like some of the neighbors. I've never seen him anywhere except behind the wheel, or in his yard with a drink in his hand.

River springs into action, stuffing things into his backpack—water, power bars, beef jerky, bug spray—then his socks and running shoes.

"What are you doing?" Harlan says.

"What does it look like?"

"You're out of your mind."

River ignores him, turning to me. "You wearing socks and running shoes?"

I nod.

"Take water, whatever food you have."

I sit there, unable to move.

"Jillian," he says, like a warning.

Harlan runs a hand through his hair. "River…" He's losing it.

"This is your last chance to turn around," River says. He looks at his dad levelly. "We can make it back to Houston in less than fifteen minutes."

"I'm not turning around. I'm not going back."

River flings open the car door. "Let's *go*, Jillian!"

I freeze.

River climbs out of the front seat. Harlan watches me through the rearview mirror.

"Good girl."

Good? More like lame. Zombie. All I'm capable of is not deciding, my life on hold. Thanks, Mom, for telling me to think for myself, but always making decisions for me.

But right now being with Harlan feels safer than leaving, so as usual, I do nothing.

River leans against the car and pulls on socks and ties his running shoes. He looks back at me searchingly as he slips his arms through the straps of his backpack. I'm out of time.

Decide. Decide. Decide.

I grab the plastic handle over the door and squeeze so hard it should splinter in my sweaty hand.

"Stay where you are." My mom's words echo in my head. She'll be furious if I go. I stare back at River. He shakes his head, giving up on me, and breaks into a run.

Something explodes inside me when he leaves, my whole body vibrating inside, like I'm in overdrive. Am I panicking for him running off on his own, or me staying behind? Is he wrong to go? Am I wrong to stay? I've never had to make a decision like this. There's no one to call, no search engine with answers to help me make a decision that could kill me or keep me alive. What do I do? Where do I go for help?

I sit still. The car doesn't move. Time is suspended. We are locked in the middle of a major highway with nothing around us except shuttered commercial buildings and now-vacant warehouses on empty streets. How safe is it to be stuck in a car? High winds can shatter glass and even lift the SUV and send it flying. There are giant road signs. What if the wind tears them down and sends them soaring like missiles across the freeway, slicing us up like giant blades? Do we just sit still and wait to be hit?

I think of the pictures in the Houston Science Museum of the figures in ancient Pompeii covered in volcanic ash. What would it feel like to be buried alive? One second your everyday life was in motion, everyone around you was alive, and things happened as usual. A nanosecond later, without warning, Mount Vesuvius erupted and the world turned into a diorama of the dead, buried underneath a shroud of volcanic ash.

My whole body is pumping out sweat, and it's not just the heat in the car. I try to breathe deeply, to take myself to a calmer place, but I can't. I can't. I feel like I have a blown-up heart pounding in my chest. My head is foggy, blood rushing in my ears.

I stare at Harlan through the mirror. I thought he'd get out of the car to see which way River ran, but he didn't. He sits there defiant, staring ahead, neck muscles taut. Doesn't he care? "Do you want to move up front?"

His voice startles me. "Sure." I open the back door and get out to study the unending panorama of cars in rows, everything still, like we're all frozen in time. I get into the front seat and slam the door. Harlan nods his head in approval.

The weather isn't holding still. The air is thick and heavy as if the rain above us is enclosed in a massive swollen cloud, waiting for a pre-ordained moment to burst and come cascading down.

"Do you want a snack or something to drink?" he asks.

"No...thanks."

I look down at my hands. They're trembling. Does he see? He doesn't seem to.

"It'll start moving," he says, stiffly.

I don't answer.

From somewhere inside, I hear myself say, "I...I can't stay."

"What?"

In the distance, I can still see River running. "I can't stay. I think he's right. We're going to die if we stay here. It's wrong. It's a mistake."

He sits there, not answering.

"You should turn around, go back. There's still time." I wait for him to answer, but he doesn't. He just shakes his head back and forth, staring in front of him.

I tie my running shoes and then pull out my phone and text River, pushing the car door open.

"*Wait!*"

PART 2

CHAPTER 12

12 HOURS TO LANDFALL

RIVER

No time to talk. We run, hydrate, and keep running, running, and running, stopping to dig pebbles and dirt out of our shoes, then running more, back toward Houston, the way we came. We're next to each other, but on our own, like strangers in a race. I've done miles, marathons before, so I'm used to this. But she isn't. She's winded, struggling. I watch her from the corner of my eye. Sympathy isn't going to help. I look away thinking about everything else.

"I don't know how much longer I can keep…"

Shut up and keep going. I stay silent.

"You're used to running in the heat, you're in good condition…"

After I came back, I started running again. Every day, any weather, in spite of it. Heat, rain, steam-room humidity, my fuck-you fitness regimen, jumping hurdles, the ones in front of me for the rest of my life. I couldn't change my head, but I could change my body, build hardness, and toughen my heart. I'd become somebody else. Peak fitness or die.

"I have to stop," she says, nearly gasping for breath.

I don't hear her, I'm deaf. I won't play to that. Suck it up.

"River...*River!*" She grabs my arm and shakes me.

I glance up at the darkening sky. "Two minutes."

We're on a side street parallel to the highway going against the traffic in an industrial part of town where no one would choose to be. A body shop off to the left, a taqueria, a McDonald's. Warehouses with their protective steel doors down, the outsides zigzagged with bloodred and green graffiti. This is a giant ghost town now. No one's around except for the victims in their cars on the highway. The sky fades from light to dark and then brightens again, as if the sun can't make up its mind. She drops her backpack and is about to sink down when I see them.

"Not there!" I grab her arm and jerk her away, just in time.

"What? What is it?"

"Fire ants."

There are mounds of them. I kick one of the small hills of sand and it rears up, tiny red ants poking out, springing to life, like an army erupting from a hidden bunker, scattering in all directions, running for cover. I learned about them the hard way. My first week in Texas I was outside in sandals and stepped on an anthill. The next morning I was covered with hellish red bites.

We stop at a clearing farther away and finally drop down. I take out half a pill and tilt my head back.

"Stop taking those," she says. "You're going to pass out!"

I look at her and don't answer.

JILLIAN

I finally sink down. I didn't think it would be this hard.

River looks at his phone. "Traffic's moving, my dad says." He shakes his head. "So what, now we run back and it stands still? No way I'm going back."

I couldn't if I wanted to. "Any idea where we're going to hide out once we're back in Houston?"

He pats his pocket. "I have the key to the school."

I tilt my head to the side. "Why didn't you tell your dad that?"

"Are you kidding?"

I wait for him to explain, but he doesn't.

"How did you get it?"

"Briggs gave us keys so we could get into the locker room when the school was closed."

"That was allowed?"

He raises an eyebrow.

"He never asked for it back?"

"Never had a chance..."

"I don't understand..."

He waves his hand dismissively.

It never occurred to me to take shelter in the school. It was a brick building. It looked like a fortress. It was way better than sitting inside a car on the freeway. "There are juice machines and probably food in the kitchen. Of course, we could be accused of breaking in."

"You think they'll be looking for prints after a hurricane?" River gets to his feet. "Let's get going. A few more miles. You ready?"

Is there's a choice?

I once read about an ultra marathon in California, a 135-mile race in July across Death Valley where temperatures are over 120 degrees. They say it's the world's toughest foot race. It goes from below sea level in

Death Valley up to Mount Whitney, over 14,000 feet high.

I never understood who ran those races or why. Maybe guys like River, who needed to jump hurdles and test themselves. They needed victories in their lives to prove that they were strong and could overcome hardship. Or maybe it was about distraction, when everyday life didn't offer you challenges and you needed to up the stakes to feel alive again.

This isn't Death Valley, but it feels like it. I think about that race as I stay in motion, slowing only to sip water before catching up to River. Suddenly I get a cramp, like a knife in the side of my hip. I stop and lean over. I can't move. He glances behind him then runs back. "Blow out and rub it." I try it, and it eases up. We keep going.

He never asks how I'm doing. He keeps going, oblivious to me. Finally I slow down again.

"I'm so thirsty and tired." I can't help myself. I'm not a stoic. I can't pretend to be.

"I didn't force you to come."

No...

He looks off annoyed, then turns back to me. "You can do it."

"How do *you* know?"

He looks back at me coldly. "Because you have no goddamned choice."

My head throbs and every joint is burning, but rage or resolve propels me to keep moving. I think of River's tattoo.

Never. Give. In.

I force myself to keep going, trying to understand why this is all happening. If logic's gone, what's left? I consider karmic payback because this is the first time I ignored my mom and ran off. Sari used to call me Miss Goody-Goody because I never got into trouble like other kids in school. I always studied when I had to. My grades were good, I never did drugs or drank much. But now everything was out of my control.

My cell rings: my mom again. I drop the phone into the bottom of my backpack and run faster. I'm furious at her now—for abandoning me, for telling me what to do when she was on another planet. If it wasn't for her, I wouldn't be running a half marathon in weather so hot it can stop your heart.

CHAPTER 13

10 HOURS TO LANDFALL

RIVER

It's raining now, a soft, steady downpour before the real show when the streets turn into streams. A granola bar and a liter of water, my Danielle diet. So what? I'm used to semi-starvation. That's something you get good at when you're locked away. It beats rancid food and nights with your head in the toilet, upchucking your guts, convinced you're dying.

"What's the matter, hotshot, you don't like hamburger meat mixed with worms?" The night guard stood at the bathroom door watching me heave again and again. He laughed. *"I wouldn't feed the shit they give you to my dog."*

Then he'd go back to his desk and unpack the food he brought from home. He'd enjoy eating it in front of us, making a show of wiping the steak sauce from his mouth with his clean, white napkin.

With my shaking hands, I slice the top off my water bottle with my knife and hold it out to catch rainwater.

JILLIAN

Kelly calls. "How boring is this?"

Boring?

"Jillian, you there?"

"Yeah." I try to pretend I'm not out of breath.

"What's wrong?"

"Why?"

She doesn't answer. "How far ahead of us are you?"

No way to fudge this. "I'm not."

"What do you mean?"

"I left. I ran from the car."

"Jill, what are you talking about?"

"I left…with River. We didn't think we'd make it on the highway."

"Are you crazy?"

"I'm getting there."

"Where are you going?"

"Back. To Houston."

"What the hell?"

"You're wasting your power," River says, trying to grab my phone.

I pull it away. "Don't! Kel, I'll call you back."

"Where in Houston? Tell me Jill! Stay on the phone!" She sounds scared. I've never heard that in Kelly's voice before, and now it scares me. But I can't tell her where we're going. I disconnect.

I reach into my backpack for a juice. Only six of twelve boxes left and two packs of peanut-butter crackers. Stupid to eat those, they're dry, but you don't exactly make smart food choices when you're starving.

My body feels horse-whipped from the run, everything red, blistered, achy, and swollen, my feet bologna-sized, the body's way of saying, "Take a look at how you're destroying yourself." Oily sweat covers my skin. I must glow like I'm radioactive. I tear at flying strands of hair blindfolding my face.

Whoosh! I lose my balance and pitch forward, landing in mud. "Shit!" I manage to pull myself up then slip again, my eyes tearing up. My legs, shorts, and hands are coated with mud. River glances over, but does nothing. I give up trying to wipe the filth away and rake my hands along the sides of my T-shirt.

I. Am. A *filthy pig*. Then I work to wipe my mind of that. It won't help. *K-e-e-p g-o-i-n-g.*

I say it over and over to drive the mantra into my brain.

Block everything and keep going. I do until I'm shaken out of self-hypnosis by a deep ache in my ankle. To make it worse, the wind is now sending me sideways, moving like a crab. I lean against a tree by the side of the road, my legs sinking, unable to support me anymore.

I slip down to the ground, landing in a mud puddle. It feels so good to stop, to rest. I lean my head back. How insane to run when I never trained.

"What?" River says, stopping next to me, his face in a hard line.

"I'm...dead."

His face darkens. "It's not much farther, you can make it."

I shake my head back and forth. "I can't." I turn away so he won't see the tears. Is this heatstroke?

My dad tried to run the marathon one year. He never made it because at mile twenty he hit the wall, his legs turned to jelly. They wouldn't support him anymore. That's what this is. The breaking point. My absolute limit. All I care about is sleeping, every part of me aching for rest, crying for help.

"You can," River insists, his face hardening.

"Just go, OK? Don't worry about me."

"I'm not going."

"Why do you even care?"

He stares back at me and doesn't answer, a muscle in his jaw pulsing.

"Go, River. Just go! Leave me alone." He turns his back on me, but stands there, a hand on his hip.

I close my eyes and feel myself drifting.

"C'mon," he says, waking me, his voice softer.

I shake my head.

"Jillian!"

"I can't."

He kneels down in front of me. "C'mon, we're losing time."

It takes too much energy to answer.

"Jillian," he says, again.

I close my eyes.

"You *can*," he hisses. He slaps me hard across the face. "Move. Now!" Smack! He slaps me again.

"Stop it," I scream, reaching out to grab his hand, but he pulls it back then slaps me again, harder this time, my skin stinging from the blows.

"Get up, get up now!"

"No!" I try to cover my face and head with my hands, fury rising up in me. He is crazy. Aidan tried to warn me, why didn't I listen? Maybe that's why he got locked up, for beating people up and bullying them.

"You're coming," he says, his teeth clenched. "Just decide you want to." He pulls my arm roughly and tries to pull me up. "Let's go."

I refuse to budge. I can't.

"Jillian," he says, like a warning.

"Why don't you take out your knife and cut my throat? You probably killed someone before, right? Maybe you're used to that now."

94

"Christ!" he says, looking away, shaking his head. He shifts, as if he's about to go, then turns back to me.

"I never killed anyone," he says, looking at me coldly. "But I probably should have." He grabs my arm. "Up, now."

I wipe my burning eyes with the back of my filthy hands and start walking again, working at catching my breath, feeling it travel down my scorched throat and lungs. I try to focus on each individual step, every one a triumph. One. Another. Then another. Not how far to go, but the distance growing shorter with every step.

Shorter, shorter, shorter, shorter. I keep saying the words over and over in my head. *Shorter, shorter, shorter,* obsessed by the repetitive sounds, blocking distraction—heat, sweat, the drawing pain in my feet and legs, every diverting thought...*shorter, shorter, shorter. Shorter, shorter, shorter.*

Before I can say anything, River turns down a side street and starts to try the doors of one car after another. I run after him. "What are you doing?" He looks at me and looks away. "Stealing a car?" No answer.

I don't want to get in trouble. But to get us moving faster...and not to have to run anymore. On his fifth try, he finds an old dented Chevy just outside a body shop.

"Bingo." He laughs. "And the key is in the ignition. Perfect. Get in," he says, climbing into the driver's seat.

I'm on autopilot, locking my seat belt and staring ahead. He drives down the empty street as the rain suddenly starts to hit harder, pounding on the roof. I've seen these flash floods before in Texas. In minutes the streets turn into wading pools.

River finally gets onto the entrance ramp down to the freeway. So few cars. Everyone is already gone now, and if they're not, they're at home, staying put.

Except us.

Then I look up and see waterfalls. I scream.

They're cascading down the high barriers on both sides of the freeway, pouring down like Niagara. But by then we're already on an exit ramp going into a shallow lake. We plunge in and begin to float. The water level around us rises and within seconds it reaches the tops of our tires and laps at the hood of the car as we move.

"We have to get out of here." My voice comes out strained, pleading.

River looks around him, running a hand through his hair. "We'll power through," he says. "It's still moving, we're not flooded out yet."

Somehow the car keeps churning ahead, only I'm not sure if the water is carrying us or it's the engine that's taking us forward. The water sloshes over the windshield, again and again.

"Jesus," he mutters as we continue to go forward. Then suddenly I lose my bearings, I don't even remember where we are and I freak, hypnotized by the red rosary beads hanging off the windshield mirror, swinging back and forth violently as the wind shoves the car around roughly. I reach out to grab the beads and they break, spilling down over the floor of the car.

"Oh my God, River, what did you do? What's happening?"

"I didn't do anything!" he says. "It's a goddamned hurricane! Stay calm, OK? Just stay calm. We're almost there."

"Almost there? We're going to drown in this, Jesus, why did we do this?"

"Calm down, OK?"

My heart feels like it's going to break through my chest. River concentrates on driving, his face as taut and expressionless as his dad's was.

The wind-driven water wallops the car from side to side as the rain hits the roof as hard as golf ball–sized hail. If the car tips, we could get stuck inside. River grips the wheel with both hands, trying to steady it.

Somehow we emerge from the lake. "Pray the motor isn't totally flooded out," he says. "C'mon babe," he whispers to the car. The water around us starts to recede. Miraculously, the car keeps going.

He laughs, almost to himself. "Can't believe this old heap is still working. See?"

I bite my lip to keep from telling him to go to hell.

Then a rush of water surrounds us as if a dam broke. It starts to fill the car. Within seconds, it's over our knees.

"Omigod, we're going to drown!"

"Unbuckle your seat belt, quick!" River yells.

"What?"

"C'mon," he yells, pushing out his door, despite the wall of water pressing back against it, like it's trying to drown us. He manages to get it open and I slide over. Waist-high water surrounds us.

"What are you doing?"

"We'll swim up to the exit ramp," he says, out of breath. "And walk from there."

With my heavy wet bag on my back nearly weighing me down, I swim after him, stroke by heavy stroke, the water smacking my face like I'm swimming against the tide. I'm sucking air, water splashing up into my face, every stroke an effort against the force of the water against us. *You're saving someone's life*, I keep repeating, pretending I have to reach a drowning kid.

River swims ahead of me, every so often glancing back to look at me. *You bitch, Danielle, you bitch*, I keep repeating to myself, anger fueling me, keeping me going, stroke after stroke until I'm closer. We make our way toward the side of the road, and finally we're at the ramp going up. The water is only as high as our ankles as we finally get out.

"Holy shit," he says, breathless.

I'm breathing so hard I can't answer.

"We're not far now," River says. "Just a block or two."

My sneakers are waterlogged, like weights on my exhausted legs. Just a block or two. If I can make it.

RIVER

I have to pull her along, but we get to the school. The wind's blowing crazy hard, the whipping rain flooding the streets, nearly knee-high now, gusts slapping our faces, but finally we're at the back door of the school.

I never thought I'd be here again.

I flash back to the late day practices. It was dark out, we weren't supposed to be there, but we had keys and let ourselves in. We went out to the field and practiced, then we came in and talked strategy. If it went well Briggs ordered pizzas. If not, we stayed hungry.

The strangest thing was that every day at exactly 6:15, Briggs would stop practice. Without a word, he'd walk back into the building for five minutes. We wondered what the hell he was doing.

Then one day one of the guys went to the bathroom, passing Briggs's office during that five-minute break and the mystery came clear. Briggs went inside to feed the canary. Something about the rigidity of that schedule freaked me out.

After practice I'd drive home at eight or nine, stopping for fast food. Then there was homework. I crashed for five or six hours and the next day it started all over again.

"Hope they didn't change the lock." Jillian stares at me in disbelief.

I fish for the loose keys in my soaking hip pocket. Finally I slide one out. I reach for the handle. "Start praying."

"That should help."

"I got you here, didn't I?" She's finally quiet. "You're free to run back to my dad's car at any time, OK? Don't worry, I won't stop you now. You won't be stuck here with me." I take a deep breath, and insert the key.

It doesn't fit.

She's breathing hard. I look over at her. *Don't say it.*

I jiggle it and then struggle to pull it out, finally. I turn it over and try again. I know what she's thinking. I'm not crazy. And no, it's not the goddamn pills.

It still doesn't fit.

"Crap." I pull the key away and search my pocket for the right one. I used to know it by the grooves, but my mind is dead now. I flatline. I forget things. Everyday things. I take out another one and as I'm about to insert it, it slips from my wet, shaking hand, sinking into the pool of swirling mud covering my sneakers.

"Omigod," she says.

We drop to our knees searching.

Things don't just disappear, where the hell could the damn key have gone? The rain is pelting our backs, dripping over our heads like we're under faucets. In seconds, it could have floated ten feet away. Tree branches snapping from the live oaks are airborne, smacking our backs. And this isn't even Danielle yet, it's just a hint of what's to come.

JILLIAN

I sift the mud through my fingers. A key doesn't disappear. It's here somewhere. I rake through the dirt again and again.

"We'll find it," River says, almost to himself.

I look up at the building with its brick façade and red steel doors. The wind gusts are smacking the American flag, pushing it back and forth. Shouldn't they have taken it down to protect it? Where was the custodian?

This isn't my school now, it's a refuge. I look at the overhang above the door and the covered walkway. Where would we hide if we couldn't get inside? In the giant stinking metal trash containers they use for garbage after renovation work? An unlocked car somewhere? A house that someone forgot to lock? We left his dad because the freeway wasn't safe.

Some of the houses across the street are boarded up. Is anybody home in any of them? Would they open their doors to us if they were? If we can't get into the school we'll have to break in somewhere, but how, with our bare hands? It's not like people are hiding in their basements to protect themselves here. There are no basements in Houston, except for the buildings downtown and some of the houses in River Oaks, one of the wealthiest parts of the city. The ground is too marshy. I look at my watch. Nearly six o'clock About two more hours until it gets dark.

"Ow!" A thick branch flies by and whips my arm, scraping it, leaving me bleeding.

River doesn't even look up. He keeps searching through the mud, fixated, oblivious, picking up clumps of it and letting it run through his fingers. I go back to doing the same thing. Five minutes go by, and then ten, and we can't find it anywhere. The only things I sift out of the mud are stones and bloated, gelatinous worms that I fling away.

We're on our knees in filthy, soaking wet clothes, sweat mixed with rain dripping down our faces. Yard garbage is now airborne as we search, hands buried in mud that draws us in like quicksand.

"We have to get inside somewhere."

River ignores me.

"It can't end this way, it can't," I say. I might as well be talking to myself because he doesn't answer. "After we left the car and came all the way back here."

I look all around. What do we do? Where do we go? I get up to start looking for someplace, anyplace to hide.

"Got it," he says, finally, pushing a wet tangle of hair away from his eyes with the back of his hand. He gets to his feet and tries the key again.

It doesn't work.

"River…"

"Be quiet, just be quiet, OK?"

I bite my lip. He inhales deeply as he struggles to work the key out of the lock. Is it jammed in now? He gets it out then flips it over, trying it again.

A heavy click. The key turns over. Finally.

"Yes!" His face relaxes. He pushes, but the door doesn't give. Nothing. Why? What's wrong? He tries again, pushing with the heel of his hand. Still nothing.

How can that be?

He presses his shoulder against it and pushes harder. It doesn't budge.

"What…?"

"Stand back!" He steps away and then runs up, hurling his entire weight against it. There's a frightening creak as though wood is being split apart, but the door gives way.

He heads into total darkness, and I follow him.

CHAPTER 14

8 HOURS TO LANDFALL

JILLIAN

We've entered a tomb. Hot, stagnant air envelops us in the darkness. It's hard to breathe. River slams the door and grimaces, nearly pitching to the floor.

"What, what is it?"

He leans over, bracing himself with his hands on his knees, his mouth open. He takes a deep breath, his eyes closed. "Just...dizzy." When he finally stands up again he rubs his shoulder and tries to move it. "Ow, God," he moans, squeezing his eyes shut, but he manages to stay upright. He takes a deep breath and keeps walking.

Is it broken? Fractured? It has to be bad, considering the way he threw himself against the door. How can I help him? What can I do? I follow him along the dark hallway to the gym, our mud-soaked sneakers squishing with every step, as if an invisible tribe of ghouls were trailing us.

I'm struck by the absolute silence. The surround-sound conversations, laughter, shrieking voices, band rehearsal music, locker doors slamming—all of the cacophony of everyday school sounds—are absent now.

"Back in school."

River's voice startles me. The bitter edge. His eyes search the corridor like a cop ready for whatever might come at him from behind a closed door. I follow him into the gym and then behind it into the locker room. He flicks a light switch. The neon lights go on with a low buzzing sound.

"Still power," he says. "Unreal."

He walks along the rows of blood red lockers, and then stops and falls silent, staring at one in front of him with no lock.

"Was that yours?"

He doesn't seem to hear me. A moment later he kicks the door and then kicks it again, harder, cursing under his breath.

"River, *stop*! You're scaring me."

He turns to me abruptly, as if he realizes for the first time that I'm there.

"Let's get out of here. We can go to the gym and get mats," he says. "We need to sleep."

But first we stop at the water cooler, taking cup after cup of water until we can't drink any more. The water cooler is nearly empty when we stop. River stares ahead for a few seconds, lost in thought, before turning away. As he's about to shut the lights, he gives the locker room a last glance over his shoulder.

We stop in the bathrooms and then go to the gym. Shafts of gray late-afternoon light filter through the gym windows. They reach almost to the ceiling, maybe fifteen feet high, protected by metal gates. Even if the glass shatters, only splinters can get through.

River pulls two blue plastic mats from the top of a pile against the wall and tosses them on the wooden floor near the wall farthest from the window.

"I'm wiped," he says, dropping his backpack. He kicks off his sneakers and slides his wet T-shirt over his head, then unbuttons his muddy jeans, yanking them down and stepping out of them. His shoulder is already streaked red and purple like a tattoo gone wrong. I look away. He leaves on his shorts, and then spreads his clothes on the floor to dry. "When we get up we can hunt for food."

River eases down and stretches out on the mat. He turns away from me, groaning when his shoulder touches the mat. He needs ice, painkillers, but we have nothing, and we're too exhausted now to search anyhow. I peel off my wet, mud-caked shorts, but leave my tank top on. Every muscle inside me is quivering, too stressed and exhausted to relax. I turn one way and then the other, my hip bone jabbing into the hard mat, skin sticking to the plastic. My deodorant gave up hours ago.

I lie there with my hands tucked under my head. How will I know when we're in the worst of it? Will the walls crash in, or is the building strong enough to withstand it?

As if in answer, the wind whistles at a higher pitch as it forces itself through the branches of the trees. Crack! An arm of a tree breaking off. I sit up, on high alert, pressing my fingers into my ears.

"River?"

No answer.

All I want is to be home. A clean bed, my shower, and the AC so cold I need a sweatshirt. I lie down again, shifting from side to side. Am I asleep or awake? I'm so hot I feel faint. My body jerks. I dream the dream I've had over and over, a replay of when I was I five and I fell off the handlebars of my cousin's bike and fractured my ankle. The nightmare nests in my brain like the one about the hurricane that leaves me gasping for air.

Victim.

I'm always a victim. I shift again and start to close my eyes when lightning illuminates the gym like a lightbulb exploded. I stare at River's back for a few seconds before the gym goes black again. Now I know what I saw. A scar across half his back. I close my eyes and start to slip into sleep, but I'm jerked awake by more thunderclaps.

"River?"

Say something, anything—that you're not afraid, even if you don't mean it. Anything. I'm scared.

I lean over him to look at his face. Despite the explosions, he's deep asleep, breathing softly and evenly. I reach into my waterlogged backpack and search until I find him: Cubby, my teddy bear. His chocolate-colored fur has worn off now, and he's bald in spots from years of cuddling, but that doesn't matter. I tuck him under my cheek, inhaling his familiar musty smell.

"Cubby." It's comforting to whisper his name in the dark. I used to talk to him like he was my worry doll, and he took in my words silently— the keeper of all my secrets—always there for me. I lean against his soft stomach, exhaustion spreading through me, and drift off.

Something—not the storm—wakes me. Talking. Where is it coming from? We're in total darkness except for flashes of lightning.

River.

A lightning flare bathes him in brightness for a split second. I sit up. Another crash of thunder and splintered light. A voice. What am I hearing?

He's talking, but not to me. In his sleep?

"No!" He turns away, upset, muttering. He sits up breathing hard,

spilling outside the lace edge of a pink bra. L
ay quickly, my breath catching.

ever to pull on my filthy jeans with one arm, tr
ulder still. The jeans are damp and mud-caked
ake my way down the corridor.

e. My head floods with memories. I lean against th
I haven't eaten, maybe that's it, low blood sugar. C
ugh me, my heart punching as the memories come

elf to keep walking. I stop at the science room
opical Storm Allison pictures up on the walls sho
ed into a nightmarish Waterworld. Focus. I try to
g pain in my shoulder throwing me off balance.
r, supplies. Food, water, supplies. Focus.

through closets. Nothing. I go through the teac
I take four and chew them up, then stuff the bottle
A portable radio. That's a start. The jarring sound
e.

of Hurricane Danielle still...static...offshore, but a se
ded with—" The radio rumbles with static. "...and s

ce is familiar. Jesus...Jillian's mom. "...filled with cry
d barking dogs, continues to jam the freeways as hundr
ds of residents of the Gulf Coast make a last-ditch ef
" It cuts out. "...the storm approaching category four is
nd appears to be heading for landfall...between...Hous
tropolitan area...

gridlocked exodus, estimated to include some 1.8 milli
fanning the flames of anger and resentment among reside
questioning whether the planning for this giant evacuation w

his hands locked around his bent knees, staring ahead. As if in slow motion, he reaches for his jeans on the floor and slides the knife out of the pocket. Click. He targets something ahead of him with the point of the blade.

BOOM! Rattling thunder! BOOM! Another explosion like a cannon blast. I startle. River doesn't even hear it. He takes aim. I can't take my eyes off him. He turns and reaches over to me suddenly, grabbing my wrist tightly, his face inches from mine.

"I'm not going to tell you again, OK?"

I'm fixated on the tip of the knife, inches from my face. I try to pull back, but he tightens his grip and won't let go.

"River." I try to shake free, to wake him. "You're having a bad dream. Let me go—it's Jillian!"

Seconds go by. Does he hear me? He releases my arm. His body goes slack. The hand with the knife falls away, only he doesn't wake. He sits staring ahead, transfixed by the visions in his head. He's asleep, in a trance. I'm walled out; he can't hear me. I hold my breath, watching him. He folds the knife and puts it down next to him. He lies back, his eyes close. In seconds his breathing becomes soft and regular again.

He was asleep the whole time.

Now *I* can't sleep. I take out my dream catcher and put it on the floor between us, like that might make a difference now. What I really need is a Saint Christopher medal.

CHAPT

2 HOURS

RIVER

I force my eyes open. How long di
through me as I turn, and it all co
swollen, burning inside. Probably a

Sweat dries, blood clots, bones he

One of my dad's marine corps slc
up. I walk to the window.

Daylight. The sky is a ghostly gree
seen this color outside before. An unea
looks like I'm inside another galaxy. Ju
now. In the distance there's a faint rumb

I walk toward Jillian. She's curled up
a stuffed toy, red hair everywhere, her lips

swell of her breas
panties. I turn aw

It takes me fo
keep the bad sho
doesn't help. I m

Briggs's offic
to brace myself.

Fear surges thr
Goddamn him.

I force mys
the framed Tr
Houston turn
out the searin

Food, wat

I search
desk. Advil.
my pocket.
human voic

"...force
cars overloa
on—"

The vo
children ar
of thousar
to reach...
building
whose me

"The
people, i
who are

adequate"—again, static interrupts—"Governor and the military are preparing to aid stranded vehicles."

Then something about the eye of the storm, a few miles wide in diameter. I think of the unsettling color of the sky. The quiet before…

And my dad? Is he still sitting there in the driver's seat, waiting? When would it dawn on him…I turn it off. Don't think about him. What good will it do? I go from room to room looking for anything useful before ending up in the kitchen. I find juice boxes and oatmeal cookies. Enough to fill our stomachs, for now.

JILLIAN

It's light. Morning? I turn to look for River. He's gone.

"River?" My fluttering heart registers his absence before my brain. This is my school, I know my way around, but that doesn't matter now. "*River?*"

Pain shoots through me as I stand. My feet are swollen, blistered, filthy; my red toenails encrusted with mud. My feet barely support me. I pull on my damp, filthy shorts and pad into a classroom down the hall. I stare out the window and everything inside me tightens.

We're surrounded by water, with islands of high ground strewn with toppled trees, tangles of fallen tree branches, and an odd collage of objects, from empty rubber garbage pails and children's red wagons to beaten-up bikes, garage doors, car doors, roof tiles, and slats of broken wooden fences. I watch a refrigerator float down the street. The fender of a car.

The windows aren't rattling. Silence. Is the storm over? Did it hit category 5? If it did, it wasn't nearly as bad as I expected. I snicker to myself. I have something to brag about now, surviving a cat 5 hurricane.

"I can't believe this," I say out loud, to assure myself I still have a voice. I go to the wall and check the lights. Nothing. We must have lost power overnight.

I hear footsteps behind me and I turn.

"I found this stuff," River says with a boyish grin. I smile back at him as he hands me oatmeal cookies and juice. We sit on the mats and tear at the wrappers, then stuff our faces. His jaw is shadowed by the stubble of a light beard.

"I didn't hear you get up."

"I called you, but you didn't move," he says.

"I've never been that tired in my life."

His shoulder looks worse than before, an irregular patch of deep purple. "How do you feel?"

He shakes his head dismissively. Should I tell him about his dream? Does he even know he had it? I doubt he would want to hear how I watched it happen.

"I wish we had a radio."

"I found one in a classroom." He pulls a transistor out of his backpack and looks for a station that isn't full of static.

"It's your mom."

"What?"

I hear Mom's voice. "Half of the city is without power this morning," she says. I grab it from his hand. It's like she's in the room with us, only she's not. She's the eyes and ears for the world, only I can't reach her. She does radio reports sometimes. Now she must be covering for someone who couldn't get there to do the story. It feels so odd to hear her. She has no idea where I am or that I'm listening. She doesn't know if I'm dead or alive.

Mom! I want to shout, *It's me*, but that's crazy. She's in another world, at least it seems that way.

"Overnight, the storm dropped fifteen inches of rain, flooding cars, highways, and…Wind gusts in some areas are now up to one hundred miles…in the next two to four hours. If you are at home waiting it out, do not leave your safe areas now. The eye of the storm is almost…things will get quiet again, at least for a while. As we've said before, the worst is still to come. By no means are we…"

A colleague cuts in. "Can we tell listeners what they can expect?" Crackling static drowns the answer.

"I just wanted to hear her."

River stares at me. He leans back against the wall. "Welcome to your new home."

I shut my eyes. Kelly. I have to text her back. Where is she? Still on the highway? I reach for my backpack and pull out my phone.

"Forget it," River says. "The cell towers are down."

I shake my head and stare out the window. "Did you see the sky?"

He nods.

"It's so eerie, so creepy. I've never seen anything like that."

"The eye of the storm," he says, gazing out.

"Should we go outside?"

"Why?"

"To see it up close. To know what it feels like."

He snorts. "It'll feel like Danielle is taking aim, like she's got us in the crosshairs." He pretends to target me and makes a loud popping noise as he pulls the trigger.

"Stop it." But he keeps it up, as though he's peering at me through the scope of a rifle. "How much time do you think we have until it really hits?"

"Minutes, hours. Who knows?"

I turn to the window. That deep rumbling again. River hears it too, his face changes. It's a low growl that sounds like it's coming from the center of the earth.

I jump to my feet. "Before it's too late."

River squeezes his eyes shut momentarily. "Why not?" he says. "Nothing left to lose."

CHAPTER 16

THE EYE OF THE STORM

JILLIAN

The one time I smoked a joint, Kelly was over. Ethan had gone out with Jerry. We knew they smoked because Ethan's room reeked from weed even though he left the window open. They must have been wrecked because they left a half joint burning in the ashtray.

I inhaled, then passed it to Kelly.

"Feel anything?" she said.

"Nuh uh, you?"

She shook her head, took another toke, then passed it back to me. We stared dumbly at each other, and then at the same moment began grinning stupidly at nothing and everything. The grins turned to peals of laughter as everything around us suddenly had a hilarious side that only the two of us were privy to.

I can't help thinking about that now, as River opens the door and we stand there, transfixed. His eyes are shining. We stare at each other in sync, sharing something that no one else in the world is part of, high on fear now, not weed, like adrenaline junkies or storm chasers waiting for a rush.

No rain, no wind, no anything. A mesmerizing, all-encompassing stillness, the sky a ghostly, treacherous green. Even the birds are silent. Everything alive is in retreat, in a state of suspended animation. The whole world is waiting. I look back and see small frogs stuck up against the door.

"River!"

He stands wide-eyed, taking it all in. We step through the knee-high moat surrounding the school, rainfall mixed with sewage beginning to reek. The world has been shaken, debris everywhere. As we walk through it, the unimaginable happens.

The clouds begin to part, as if a screen is opening, the backdrop on a stage set. The sky morphs from an incandescent bile green to cornflower blue. The sun breaks through.

"Could it be over?" I feel strangely giddy.

"Not a chance. That's what Danielle wants you to think. She's toying with us."

"How do you know?"

"Feel it in my bones," he says.

I look for evidence. There's an unnerving calm to the air, as if we're in another universe. I take a few steps and nearly trip over a bulging tree root that's buried underwater.

River points to a downed tree. "If we were out here when that fell we'd be buried." But it's not fear on his face, it's amazement. This is a rare living science lesson. "Look," he yells. He reaches an arm out and holds up the neck of a quivering snake that dangles down the side of his arm, past his elbow. I see black, red.

"Red touch yellow, kill a fellow; red touch black, venom lack." The crazy rhyme I learned in camp springs to mind. It isn't a poisonous coral snake, I'm sure. We studied snakes in science. Texas has more varieties than any other state in the country, and Houston is home to nearly a third of them. Only now I'm blanking. I have no idea what this one is.

It's undulating as if it would rather not be held up.

"Get rid of it before it bites you."

River reaches back like he's about to throw a javelin and pitches it, as hard as he can while trying to keep half his body from moving. We both turn away.

"It's following us." I laugh hysterically.

He slithers his fingers up my back, snake-like.

"Don't do that!"

"Do what?" he says.

We walk through the water, dipping down to steer clear of low-hanging power lines. I step up on a broken tree stump to survey what happened around us and I stop. There's a sound, like a yelp. "Did you hear that?"

He nods.

"What was it?"

"An animal," River says.

The sky is slowly changing. Time is running out. The sun's still out, but the light is fading. River hoists himself up onto the arm of a bent tree. "Whatever it is, it's here somewhere." He jumps down and heads across the watery lawn and then trips, falling on his injured side.

"Ow, Jesus," he yells.

I run over and try to help him up, but he's like dead weight. "It's broken, it's got to be," he says, squeezing his eyes shut.

"We'll bandage it to keep it from moving."

"With what?" he asks, "Your trusty first-aid kit?"

"We'll find something."

He shakes off the pain and looks around us. "Maybe if we had food we could find whatever it is and get it inside with us."

"You think it's a dog?"

"I hope not."

We walk cautiously, searching, trying to figure out which way to go. The sun retreats and the sky begins to deepen from turquoise to blue gray.

River looks at the sky, biting his lip. "We have to get inside soon."

"I'll go find something in the kitchen."

"I know where the stuff is," he says. "I'll go. I'll be fast, you look out."

I stare at the sky. "Hurry!"

What's taking him so long?

The sun is gone, blue sky replaced by clouds deepening by the minute. I take a last look around, walking carefully, trying to find whatever it was, but there's nothing. Was it our imagination? Maybe we're both going crazy. I need to find River. Now. I walk toward the school door as the wind begins to whip my face. I pull it open and scream.

CHAPTER 17

JILLIAN

River is slumped down on the floor, a few feet from the door, his eyes closed. Did he pass out? Is he dead? Near his opened hand I see packages of crackers.

"River?" I rush up to him and kneel down

No answer.

"God, please!" My heart is about to burst through my chest. I reach for his left wrist, pressing it with my index finger. I can't find a pulse, nothing. I try his right wrist. Still nothing. Maybe it's me. I'm not doing it right. My hands are shaking. I doubt if I could tell if I felt a pulse inside him, or if the throbbing came from inside me. I breathe in and out slowly to try to calm myself then try again, on the left hand.

Then I feel it. "River?"

Nothing.

"River, answer me, please!"

I stroke his forehead, his hair. I run my fingers down his face, along his cheek. Seconds go by and he lies there, still. What do I do? What does it mean? Why didn't I take a first-aid class so I'd know what to do?

I study his face watching for something, anything. Finally he moves his head. His chest rises as he takes in a breath. His eyes open and he looks at me, dazed.

"What happened?" I whisper.

He stares at me for a few seconds as though he doesn't recognize me. "Are you OK?"

"I...don't know," he says, finally. His voice comes out hoarse, strained. He closes his eyes and opens them again. "I was running...I hit something, I lost balance or...I must have blacked out from the pain."

Do I get him up? See if he can walk? Keep him still? Act, don't panic. And what about whatever was outside? A person? An animal? We don't have long, whatever was out there will die without us.

"I'm OK," he says. "Did you find anything?"

"What?"

"Outside, did you find anything?"

"No. We have to stay inside. There's no more time, River." There's a low rumbling outside, like a warning, then a flash of lightning. "It's already too late...we shouldn't—"

"Help me up," he says, drawing his knees toward his chest.

"Can you stand?"

He grimaces as he pushes himself up with one hand and gets to his feet. "I'm OK."

But he's not. He's pale. He takes a step, but he's unsteady. I grab his arm. What if he passes out again? Or hits his head?

"Let's go out," he says. "We'll look fast."

"River, you can't. I don't want you to—"

"—I'm OK," he insists. "One last look, then we'll come back. If it's a dog, we can't leave him out there to die."

I push the door open and we go out, stepping carefully. He can't fall, not again. I hold him around the waist to try to support him. I expect him to protest, but he doesn't. That scares me more.

The wind is gusting hard, strong enough to knock us down, the rain pelting us from all directions, slapping at our faces. We make it down to the spot where we heard the sound, looking everywhere, calling out, but there's nothing around us that's alive, nothing.

"We've got to keep looking," I say. And then I stop. A black dog, some kind of terrier mix, I think. He's floating in the water. We're too late.

"God," I cry, pressing my hand over my mouth. I go over to him and touch his head, his fur wet. His eyes are open, but he's so pathetically still. He didn't stand a chance outside.

I'm flooded with memories of Bree, our black lab, a rescue who died two years ago. Her favorite word was 'home.' She couldn't wait to get back after a walk. Where would she have ended up in the evacuation? With me? My mom?

"River, look!"

I swivel around, but it's like he doesn't hear me. There's an expression on his face I've never seen before—his eyes open wide, his lips parted.

"Holy shit!" he says, lifting his chin. I look up and freeze. Off in the distance there's an enormous funnel cloud. It's spiraling around and around madly in a dark, dusty, sepia sky.

A tornado.

And it's coming toward us.

LANDFALL

"What we heard…the vibrating…the growling sound." I struggle for breath.

"Tornadoes come with hurricanes!" River shouts.

He's alert now like nothing happened. We start rushing toward the door, as fast as we can go without getting snared by garbage or things poking out from the ground, hidden beneath the water. But the wind is strong and it's like trying to skip through waves at the beach, the water rising up, choppy in the wind, slapping back at us. The ground is slimy and slippery. My eyes dart down and up, down and up. The sky has grown smoky and dark, as though we're looking at the world through a charcoal filter. The rumbling gets louder and deeper. We're feet from the door when the loop of my sneaker lace catches on something. I'm jerked back and lose my balance, falling and smashing my face against the sharp side of a thick tree root that's buried under the water.

"Ow, God!" It stabs my cheek like a knife. Blood spouts out over my shirt. I pull myself up, out of the water.

"Inside," River shouts, grabbing my arm and running, ignoring everything. "Now!"

We rush through the door and make our way into the hot gym as the high-pitched keening gets louder and deeper, rattling the window frames like a phantom screaming at the glass.

"Grab the mats!" River says as we run toward the supply closet. I pull them behind me as we stop at the door in the back of the gym. He fumbles for the key and finally unlocks it. I slam the door behind us, and we crouch down, the mats over our heads in the darkness, the water covering our knees. River grunts in pain from the pressure on his shoulder.

"Start praying," he says, as the roar grows louder and louder, as if we're crouching near the railroad tracks as a fast-moving freight train speeds toward us.

I bury my head under my arms, eyes shut tight, my breathing ragged, sweat pouring off me. Horrid thoughts bombard my brain from every direction. I can't process them: the roof being ripped off, everything inside the school getting sucked into the air, both of us getting buried alive under the rubble, dying for no reason like that pathetic dog, not seeing my family again ever, never living another minute. Life being ripped away without time to think or plan. Every cell inside me pulsates, electrified, trying to keep pace with the thoughts firing in my brain like shock waves.

Please, let it pass us. Spare us, please. I'll live differently, do better, anything. My ears pop. My mouth is so dry that I can barely swallow. We hold still sweltering under the mats, waiting.

Time stops. Five minutes. Ten. I can't tell. The world is upside down. The roar grows louder and louder. My head pounds. I press my fingers into my ears, but it's useless. It feels like my eardrums are bursting.

And then the roar slowly diminishes, as if it's receding into the background.

The tornado moved on. Or dissipated, replaced by nothingness.

I hold still, afraid to move. The loudest sound now is me gasping for air, trying to take a deep breath. I push the mat off my head and sit up. "It must be gone."

"I'm not ready to look," River says, exhaling, sweat dripping down his face.

My thighs feel wet. I reach down. Blood. It's everywhere.

CHAPTER 18

THE EYEWALL

JILLIAN

I press my hand against my face. The cut is deep, the blood keeps trickling out, but there's nothing I can do. I press my hand against it. It has to stop.

River stares at my face, concerned, but then turns away. "I'll look around."

"Outside?" I don't want him to go.

"No, the gym, and the corridor."

"Be careful."

I sit there soaked in sweat. The bleeding finally slows, but my shorts and T-shirt are streaked with blood. Sportswear designed by a vampire.

Where is River? How long has he been gone? As if in answer, the door creaks and then opens.

"It passed over," he says, closing it behind him. "At least the building's still standing."

"We're lucky, it could have been leveled."

"Lucky so far. The tornado passed over us, but we could get other ones. This is just the beginning." He comes closer. "You scared?"

"I...I don't know."

"You should be."

I walk into the gym, the real world again. The wind is kicking up again, blowing from all directions, shaking the windows. A metal pipe of some kind must have come loose because now there's a banging sound as if something heavy is being slammed again and again on an outside wall. We're in an enclosed brick building, but the sounds are almost unbearable. I think of River's dad, Ethan and Jerry, Kelly, Sari. Are they still in their cars? And my mom? Where is she now?

Walls of rain shatter like glass against the side of the school. Unless they're bulletproof, the windows are going to blow. As if in answer, I hear glass shattering somewhere in the building and things smashing on the floor. Pottery in the art room? Books in the library? Lamps? The science lab with the aquarium? What will be left of our school after Danielle is done ravaging it?

"It's like we're inside a haunted house."

River doesn't even nod.

The bathroom. I can't hold it in any longer, only I'm afraid to find it on my own. I have to. I can't be a baby. River's the one in pain. I force myself up and head for the dark corridor. I'm learning braille transport, using my hands instead of my eyes to guide me. I follow the familiar signposts—doors, bulletin boards, and display cases—along the way. When I finish in the stall I make my way to the sink. Without thinking, I turn on the faucet. There's still water! I wash my face with soap, crying out because it burns the gash on my face.

The nurse's office. If I can get in there, I might find bandages for River's shoulder and an antibiotic cream for my face. I walk down the corridor counting the doors. But when I get to the nurse's office, the door is locked. If only I could break the glass window in the door. But I have nothing to smash it with.

I head back to the gym, nearly tripping over a carton. It's the lost and found box, where kids drop off clothes. I grab as many T-shirts as I can find. We can rip them up instead of bandages. I walk back slowly, trying hard not to smash into anything.

BOOM! Overhead somewhere, an explosion. The building vibrates like a wall of windows has exploded.

"River? Where are you?"

I run down the corridor and find my way to the gym. "River?" No answer. I make a megaphone with my hands.

"River?"

Still no answer. I run down the hall to the nearest stairwell. "River?"

"Up here," he says. "Stay down there."

I can't. I have to know what's happening. I start to run up, then stop. There's a roar so loud it sounds like a bulldozer has plowed into a glass wall. I run into the corridor and look into the science lab. The aquarium! It's smashed to bits, chunks of glass sprayed everywhere. Most of the water has rushed out, the fish shot out in every direction, squirming on the floor. I step into the room trying to push aside the glass to clear a path with my hands so I can scoop them up, to try to save them.

"Don't go in there," River shouts from the corridor. He steps in and pulls me back. "You'll slice your hands up, and it won't help. It's too late." He closes the door behind us.

"It's not just this," he says, working at catching his breath. "The windows in a second-floor classroom splintered. A tree slammed into

127

them. But it's on the north side. We should be OK down here for a little while unless the rain floods us out."

Those tiny colored fish spread out over the floor—fifty tropical fish, maybe more. Most of them probably dead now. Electric yellow, neon blue, orange, green. So beautiful and some so rare. Lots of kids took care of them week after week, even coming into the school on the holidays to feed them. I try to convince myself that they wouldn't have lived long anyway, but that's not the point. This was such a senseless and stupid ending. They weren't supposed to die like that.

I watch the halting way that River walks and the unbearable sadness of everything that has happened hits me at once. The tears start, but I force myself to stop. "I found T-shirts," I shout, wiping my eyes with the back of my hand. "We can tear them up. You need to keep your shoulder from moving."

"Who said?"

"Ethan broke his arm once. I remember what the doctor told him." We stop in the corridor, and River takes out his knife. I hold a shirt and he slices through it, cutting it into strips. I tie one strip of fabric to another until I have a piece that's long enough to bind his upper arm to his chest. He stands still as I pull it around him, tying it securely. "That should help a little."

His face softens. "Thanks."

We fill our water bottles in the bathroom and then try to scope out the safest spots. We walk to the theater and pull open the red velvet curtains covering the windows. Not broken, so far. We climb the stairs to the stage and cocoon ourselves behind the heavy curtains. The red walls match the curtains, and on the back wall there is a mural of figures from Greek history and theater. This room is like a safe haven, with the feel of history around us. What Danielle can't destroy is the past.

Being here makes me think of the play the night of the picnic—and what happened afterwards in the darkness of the field.

• • •

The play was about the family of a former governor in the South who was removed from office for accepting bribes. As he was on his way to prison, his son died unexpectedly of a freak accident, convincing the governor that he was being punished for what he did.

I played the daughter, and it started with the family coming back from the funeral. The daughter finds out their house has been sold and all her things are packed away. She can't deal with losing everything at once.

"Acting isn't about dressing up. It's about stripping down and reaching inside yourself," Miss Larson said. "The word 'theater' comes from the ancient Greeks. It means 'the seeing place.' The great acting teacher Stella Adler said it's 'the place people come to see the truth about life...' So it's the actor's job to make the audience aware of who people are, what they want, and what motivates them, because in real life that's not easy to figure out."

For the picnic, we were performing a one-act play to pique interest in opening night. Despite my jittery feelings, the play went well.

"Awesome," Aidan said, rushing up to me. "I nearly cried."

My mom was teary-eyed, not that it took much to make her cry. Ethan saw me and held up this thumb, his equivalent of going overboard with praise. Kelly rushed up to me too. "You were amazing!"

"Make-believe works for me," I said.

We descended on the picnic table like locusts and then sat outside under the stars. Kelly was with Brian, a guy from a nearby high school. Sari was with Scott, the second-best basketball player after Aidan.

"Who's up for Frisbee?" Sari asked, after we all pigged out.

"I'm playing basketball," Aidan said.

"Me too," said Scott.

129

That left Bethany, Kelly, Sari, Brian, and some other kids from my grade.

"You're the star tonight, J-girl," Kelly said, tossing me the Frisbee. "You throw the first one." I tossed it as far as I could, and Brian immediately caught it.

"Wimpy," he said. "You better work out some more." He got into a pitcher's pose and then threw it over my head. It soared into the air, landing halfway across the park.

"And your point is?" I yelled, running after it.

"Out of the park," Brian yelled, breaking into a bump and grind dance. "Home run."

"Not fair," Sari said. "It's in Siberia."

Everyone scattered in different directions to search. It would have helped to have the outside of the park lit or a Frisbee that was glow-in-the-dark.

"Check over by the tennis court," Kelly said. "I'll look back in the field."

"I hope you're wearing bug spray," I said. "We'll get eaten alive."

"Not a chance," Kelly said, holding up a fist. "Texas girls are tough."

There was tall grass at the bottom of the hill. The Frisbee had probably landed down there, hidden by weedy patches that were home to mosquitoes. It was definitely dumb to keep looking there. Using my phone as a flashlight, I searched all over the ground and finally gave up. I was heading back to the others when I heard a rustling behind me. A raccoon? Something bigger? Slowly, I stepped away.

"Yaah!"

I jumped. Someone laughed and I pivoted, startled.

"River! You're always scaring me."

He waved the Frisbee over his head. "You're not looking for this, are you?"

I reached for it, but he pulled it behind him. "After."

"After *what*?"

"The kiss," he said. "I need to pay my dues."

"Excuse me?"

His face turned serious. "I thought everyone had to do that, unless the guys on the team were bullshitting the new guy."

"Oh," I smirked. "The tradition.'"

"So?" He smiled. "Initiate me."

He moved closer, tracing my bottom lip with his thumb. Before I could answer, his lips touched mine, moving back and forth, back and forth, in a slow, intoxicating tease. "Is this how it's done?" he whispered. "Or like this?" he said, pressing harder. "Tell me."

"River," I said, pleadingly, not sure why. No one had ever kissed me like that. I felt myself leaning into him as the kiss got deeper and hotter, his arms tightening around me, his tongue playing inside my mouth, meeting mine lightly at first, then more insistently. I reached up into his hair, pulling at it, inhaling the smell of his woodsy shampoo, confused by the force of my emotions.

"You smell amazing," he whispered, running his lips lightly down the side of my neck, his body against mine, wanting more. "So lemony and sweet." I was breathing hard, and I met his lips again with the same intensity, feeling wired and alive in a way I never had before. But as his fingertips traced the edge of my bra, I pulled back.

"River," I said, leaning away, my voice a hoarse whisper. "I…can't. I have a boyfriend."

"Oh yeah?" he murmured, pulling at my bottom lip, claiming it gently with his teeth.

Boyfriend. Aidan.

I couldn't.

Aidan's face flashed in my head. Cute. Reliable. Devoted to me. "Stop," I said, pushing away. I caught my breath and looked up.

And there…was Aidan.

He had appeared out of nowhere. How long had he been standing there, watching us? His face was dark, his eyes hooded. I had never seen him so angry.

"What the hell?" he said, looking at River then back at me.

"River found the Frisbee," I said. "And the tradition…" It came out worse than stupid—breathless, in a rush. I reached behind River's back and pulled it from the waistline of his jeans as if to give Aidan tangible proof that I wasn't lying. Like that might matter now.

Fury rose in Aidan's face as he stepped closer to River. I had never seen him look like that. "Keep. Your hands. Off. My girlfriend. You dick."

River looked back at him, a smirk on his face.

"Maybe you're the dick for leaving her alone while you played basketball."

That was it. Aidan flew at him, sending both of them to the ground. Aidan worked at trying to punch River in the face, again and again, struggling against River's weight, while River kept ducking, and then finally went on the attack.

It was my fault. I should never have let River kiss me. I should have stopped him sooner. If I had this never would have happened.

"Aidan, stop it. River, get off him!"

But they ignored me. River was a couple of inches taller than Aidan and had more bulk, but Aidan made up for it in wiry strength and rage. They rolled on the ground, each of them trying to stay on top and score as many punches and choke holds as they could before the other one got on top and tried to pin the other down using fists, elbows, and knees. They cursed at each other's faces in breathless rants.

"Stop it, stop it," I kept screaming. But neither of them seemed to hear me.

A crowd started to form around them, and Ryan Whyte from the football team tried to get between them and push them apart.

"Stop it, man," Ryan said to River. "C'mon, break it up." But River got out of his grip and went at Aidan again. Ryan pulled at River's shoulders, but he couldn't manage to separate them.

Finally Coach Briggs ran over and pushed his bulk between them.

"It's over," he shouted, forcing them apart with his beefy arms. They both stood away, breathing hard, glaring at each other, wiping away sweat and blood.

"What do you think you're doing?" the coach roared, glaring at River. Then he turned to Aidan with the same hard expression. "And you!"

Neither of them answered. Blood was dripping out of Aidan's nose, and he kept trying to shake it away with his hand, before coughing and spitting it out.

"You fuck," he mumbled to River.

"Fuck you," River said, stepping up to him.

"Do you want to get suspended?" the coach yelled. "Both of you?"

River shook his head.

"No, *sir*," Coach Briggs said.

"No, *sir*," River said, the slightest edge to his voice, as he wiped blood off his mouth with the back of his hand and then spat on the ground.

The coach stared at Aidan, waiting.

"No, sir."

"Then get control of yourselves and go back to the picnic." He pointed the way as if they didn't know. Aidan followed River up the hill as Coach Briggs stood there watching them.

"You OK?" Ryan said to me.

I nodded, tears streaming out of my eyes.

"You want me to take you back or drive you home?"

"No, I'm fine, really."

Coach Briggs glared at us and finally turned dismissively, following River and Aidan toward the field. I walked back holding the Frisbee, feeling stupid and responsible. The high of being in the play was gone now. I did something I shouldn't have, and I got caught. If it wasn't for me, there wouldn't have been a fight. And now River and Aidan would pay for it.

All I wanted was to be alone to think about what had just happened. Guilty, confused feelings swirled inside me. For being responsible for the fight? For kissing River? For feeling something deep and unstoppable that I never felt when Aidan kissed me? For my heart coming alive in a way it never had before? If only I knew what that flood of feelings meant. And whether they were wrong. Or right.

• • •

Aidan was sitting off by himself, leaning against a tree. Blood was still trickling from his nose, but he didn't seem to notice or care. All the guilt and unease rose up in me again when I looked at him. I handed him a wad of tissues from my pocket.

"Put pressure on it while I look for ice," I said.

He grabbed them away from me without a word.

We stayed until nine when the picnic was over. Someone from the band was fooling around and played Taps on the trumpet. It made me think of funerals. The whole night ended badly, and most of it was my fault.

• • •

Almost at the same time, everyone headed to the parking lot. As we approached Aidan's car, Lexie's high-pitched laugh pierced the quiet. "River and Lexie hooked up," I heard Sari say to Scott. "I think he was asking her about the tradition."

"So?"

"So?" she repeated. "So she's a slut."

Scott laughed. "So? Some guys like sluts."

I stopped. Aidan was so busy nursing his anger he didn't notice, or pretended not to. So River used the line about the kiss on everyone, the innocent newcomer pretending he had just heard about the tradition. I was an idiot to fall for it.

I caught up with Aidan and grabbed his arm. "I'm sorry about tonight, really." He glanced at me coldly.

"How would you feel if you saw my tongue down Lexie's throat?"

"He was fooling around and then—"

"—Fooling around? It didn't look like that to me."

We got into his car, the click, click of the seat belts locking us into separateness. River's bike roared to life nearby. Lexie was snaked around him, smiling like she was taking home the winner of the hot guy contest. River sped up next to us, and then abruptly changed lanes cutting us off. Aidan slammed the brakes. "Asshole."

River stuck out an arm and held up his middle finger before he floored the gas.

"You'll get yours," Aidan muttered.

• • •

River sits up on the stage and glances over at me, narrowing his eyes, like he's trying to read my thoughts. "I was thinking about the one-act plays," I say, and then look away. "We practiced them over and over in here." He doesn't answer. "That seems like years ago."

RIVER

It seems like years ago to me too. I try to fight it, to forget, but it all comes back to me in here. I lie back on the stage trying to find a position that doesn't hurt, working to block out the pounding of the storm.

I had early practice the day of the picnic, so I didn't have to help set it up. When I got home Jillian was pulling into her driveway. I walked over and leaned into the driver's side window, pretending I wasn't drawn by her perfume.

"Can I ask you something?"

"Sure." She pushed her hair away from her blue eyes and stared up at me.

"Tell me about the full-moon picnic."

"What about it?"

"Why do they have it?"

"For fun?"

"What do you do—'for fun'?" I said, miming her.

"The band gives a concert, and sometimes kids in their own bands play. Then there's stupid stuff like three-legged races."

"What are you doing?"

"I'm in drama and we're doing a one-act play."

"I was in drama in my other school."

"Why don't you join now?" she asked.

"I don't have much free time."

"It only meets twice a week."

"Maybe, I don't know."

"But you're coming to the picnic?" she asked.

"You think I'd pass up a free meal?"

"No, you're always starving, right?" She pulled into the driveway before I could answer.

Ever since Ryan had told me about the tradition, I was obsessed with the idea of kissing her, which was insane since she was my next-door neighbor. Plus she was seeing someone else, not that I cared. But I didn't make any decisions right then. I thought I'd see how things went.

But after everyone ate and started to play games, I saw that some dork pitched the Frisbee into the outfield, and that was an opening for me. I made an end run to get it before she did, which wasn't hard. She was alone, searching in the dark with the light from her phone when I caught her off guard. I knew she was quiet, shy, so I moved in before she could think about what was happening. I had her in my arms, and I started living out my fantasy. She was so hot, it hurt.

Christ, don't go there. It doesn't matter anymore. I glance over at her. The shorts. The same ones she had on the day after the fight with Aidan, the afternoon I visited her up in the lair after school.

I was pretty busted up. Black and blue, split lip. Nothing broken or Briggs would have strangled Aidan. I probably got Jillian in trouble with him. I had reason to feel guilty, not that I did, but that was what I wanted her to think and it gave me my excuse. But it was more than that. I just needed to get close to her again, to share the same space. Whatever, I don't know. All I did know was that I couldn't stop thinking about her and I had to know if she felt it too.

Briggs had something to do, which rarely happened, so we got out of practice. I got home early and waited until she pulled into the driveway. Don't overthink it, I told myself.

Ethan answered the door. I liked him. He was into music like I was, so we hung out together sometimes. But he knew I wasn't there to see him. I guess news of the fight spread quickly.

"She's upstairs, in the lair," he said, mockingly.

"The lair?"

"Her hideout, above her bedroom."

I went upstairs and headed toward the room with the pink and orange colors. I saw a ladder leading up to the attic and realized what he was talking about.

"Knock, knock," I said after climbing halfway up.

"River," she said, surprised. I liked it when she said my name. I felt like she was staking a claim on me. She was sitting in the corner on the carpet, the open science book in her lap.

"Permission to enter?"

She smiled and nodded.

I walked the rest of the way up and slammed my goddamn head on the pitched roof.

"Oh, I'm so sorry," she said, crawling over to me on her knees. "Are you all right? Everyone does that—I should have warned you."

I rubbed my head, pretending not to see the low-cut tank top and shorts with a drawstring tie. One pull on the string and...I felt a jolt. She was so damn close again, I...

Focus. On her face. Fragile. Delicate skin, intense eyes, and that hair, so much of it, half up, half over her shoulders, like she just got out of bed. I turned and acted interested in the lair. It looked like a tree house. The windows were nearly as high as the tops of the old trees on the front lawn. Wood-paneled walls. Grass-green carpet. All I could think about was what I wanted to do in that tight space hidden away from everybody. "Your secret hideaway?"

She shrugged. "You like it?"

"Yeah." I looked at the sleeping bag. "You sleep up here?"

"Sometimes."

I leaned over it. It had her lemony, flower smell. "Smells like you."

"What?" I pretended not to see her blush. What was I starting? Christ, I was out of control, pathetic. If I didn't switch gears I'd be...

"Listen," I said finally. "I came to—"

"—What?"

"Apologize. I'm sorry...about the picnic...and everything."

"It was my fault. You were playing me with that line about the tradition. I shouldn't have kissed you..."

"That's the part I'm not sorry about," I said, my heart amping up. I stared at her too long. Her face got pinker, and she was biting her lip.

Go home, asshole. You're a walking hard-on. It's insane to start this. She's your next-door neighbor. You don't do that if you have a brain.

"Then what?"

138

"I hope I didn't mess things up for you—with your boyfriend. I didn't mean to get you in trouble."

"I thought you were the one who would get in trouble."

"It was no big deal," I said.

"It didn't look that way."

"I've gotten my ass kicked before."

"I thought Briggs would suspend both of you."

"No way. He needs me."

"I'm sorry you got hurt, River, really." She studied my face. "You're turning yellow."

"Chicken shit?"

She smirked. "As in bruised." She reached out and gently traced the side of my jaw with her fingertips, and then grimaced. That's all it took. The lightest touch and I felt the charge everywhere. It happened whenever I was around her. Without thinking, I reached out to grab her hand, but I caught myself. "I better go—"

"—It's OK, I—"

Instead, I ran my hand along the edge of her sleeping bag, and then I stood up fast, smacking my head again like a total genius, forgetting the roof. "Jesus."

"Oh God, River, I'm so sorry, I should have warned you again." She laughed. "This is a dangerous place."

It's you, I wanted to say. But I didn't. I needed to get out of there fast.

The memories flood back to me now. It's this protected room...the storm outside...

"Let's get out of here," I say, breathing harder. "It's airless." I reach into my pocket. Four more Advil. I throw them into the back of my throat. Anything to dull the pain.

Late afternoon and the storm is ripping into us. Every part of me is on alert. Will the damn roof crash in? Will the windows burst? The gym

139

is the biggest open space, the place that looks most secure, and with the water leaking down from the corridors, probably our best bet for now. We go back there and drop onto our mats, staring out at the gray light filtering in through the windows.

"I've never felt this cut off in my life," Jillian says.

I squeeze my eyes shut. "Try being locked up."

CHAPTER 19

JILLIAN

I stare up at the basketball hoops. What if Aidan were here instead of River? A troubling feeling spreads over me. I push it out of my mind.

Aidan sat behind me in math. It wasn't destiny that put us together, it was the alphabet. Our last names both start with M.

The real reason he started liking me, I think, was because once or twice he needed the answer on a test and after he slid his foot forward and nudged mine, I moved my paper to the side of my desk. It wasn't like he was studying to be a brain surgeon. He had to keep his grades up to stay on the basketball team, so why not?

"Thanks," he whispered to me one day after class. "You saved my ass." We started eating lunch together after that.

"I cannot believe you're going out with Aidan Michael," Sari said, like he was a rock star. "He barely looks at anybody."

"We're not going out. We're just friends."

"I wish he was my friend."

"I'll introduce you."

But Aidan wasn't interested in Sari. One Friday as we were leaving school, he did ask me out.

"Let me take you out for dinner," he said. "It's the least I can do after you saved me from failing."

"Everyone thinks we're already going out," I said, "so why disappoint them?" Even though Aidan was cute, really cute, I was one of the few girls who went to the games to watch basketball, not Aidan. That was probably why he started liking me.

"I could tell you were head over heels in love with me," he said, pushing against me playfully. I rolled my eyes.

Instead of jeans and my generic white T-shirt, I actually dressed for the date: black leggings, high-heeled sandals, and a black off-the-shoulder top. I can't take credit for the outfit. Sari came over and picked it out.

It didn't feel like me. But going out on a date didn't feel like me either.

We went to a movie and then stopped for ice-cream cones. We ate them in the car with the air on, but it wasn't cold enough to keep them from melting.

"Shit," Aidan said, as a blob of chocolate ice cream landed on his shirt. I tried to wipe it away with my napkin, basically rubbing the stain in. "You're always taking care of me," he said. "That's what I first noticed about you."

"You mean the test stuff?"

"Not everyone would do that," he said. "If we got caught, both of us would have gotten detention or worse."

"It wasn't a big deal. Anyway, I have more time to study than you do."

"I don't care about studying," he said.

"What do you care about?"

"Basketball."

"And?"

He looked at me blankly. "And nothing. I want to play professionally. That's the only thing I ever wanted to do with my life. What about you?"

What did I care about? Nothing in my mind was as clear-cut. I liked working on the school paper. I liked writing articles. But a career? A direction? I had no burning ambitions. By the time you were a sophomore, you were supposed to have a clue. In just a few years, you had to major in something. Maybe I was destined to spend my life in loserdom, never knowing what kind of work would make me happy or which direction I would take.

"What I care about most at this point in time is ice cream," I said. "Chocolate, but also pistachio. And definitely in cones, sugar cones, not waffle." We both laughed. "There is one other thing, seriously."

"What?"

"Rainbow sprinkles."

"You should get your PhD in frozen desserts," Aidan said.

"Cold comfort," I said.

He drove me home and parked at the curb. The air was heavy with the syrupy scent of jasmine. We sat in the surround-sound silence, with only the steady chirp of crickets reminding us that we weren't alone in the darkness. I tried to think of something to say, but the harder I tried, the blanker my brain became. Finally, as if it took him that long to get up the nerve, he leaned over to me, his face inches from mine.

"You look so hot," he said. "I want to kiss you."

Did he think he had to ask? "OK," I laughed. Saying it felt lame.

I leaned toward him, which seemed like the thing to do. Like showing him my test paper. His lips tasted like chocolate ice cream. The kiss reminded me of when I was ten and I kissed a boy who liked me at a birthday party. What I remembered most was metal touching metal as our braces hit.

"Sweet," Aidan said, leaning away. He kissed me again, faster. We both laughed because I probably tasted like chocolate too. He looked at me as though he wasn't sure what his next move should be. I didn't know either, so I opened the car door and slid out.

"Good night, thanks." I took baby steps in my backless heels as I walked toward the house, trying not to turn my ankle. Sari had the same shoes, only she had more practice walking in them. She called them her "sex" pumps.

Had she gone that far?

I didn't think so…

RIVER

A tall window bursts, sending a blizzard of glass shards spraying the floor, covering it like gravel. We jerk to attention, covering our heads with our arms. More explosions, like artillery fire, followed by what sounds like a tree toppling over and slamming the building. I jump up and run toward the window, scattering glass around me. The sky is so dark I can't see anything. "It's like a bombing raid." I go back to the mat and reach for the orange bottle.

Last pill. I drop it into the back of my throat. Another bandwidth of sanity, but then what? Worse panic, the shakes? I know what that's like.

She stares at me. I freak her out. Better. She'll keep her distance.

"How long do hurricanes last?" she asks.

"You won't be locked up with me forever, don't worry."

"That's not what I meant, River. Why are you like that?"

"I'm not like anything," I say, suddenly pissed off. I manage to get up, the pain shooting through me whenever I move now. I head down the hallway. I'm trapped inside my head and out. There's no way out of this. No escaping my life, or who I am. I'm scared too, only I'm not sure of what. And it won't get better. Why should it?

"Come back," she shouts.

I need to wall her out. Us together, here. Another day or two and life will start over again—if we don't drown. Me alone. Blinders on. No attempts to fill the emptiness. It's who I am now. Everything I've been through ruined me. My body, my brain. I have nothing to give her, nothing to give anybody. A few more days…I can hold onto that. I'm good at waiting now. I walk down the corridor past the display cases with the trophies and the cheerleader pictures.

Lexie.

I wasn't looking for a girlfriend. I left LA, and I left Carla. I called her every few days for a month after getting to Houston, but then life interfered. The calls got further apart. So did the texts. When I found out from a friend that she started seeing someone else, I didn't care. She was fun and hot, but something wasn't there.

When we moved I was getting used to a new school and a new world, and football took up so much of my life that there wasn't much time for anything else.

But the picnic changed everything.

Lexie was the head of the cheerleaders. She seemed to turn up everywhere I went. She was hard to miss—long dark hair and a nearly perfect body from a lifetime of gymnastics. She knew how to walk and how to dress, everything either tight or loose in all the right spots. She liked me, I knew it, but I pretended not to notice at first. Maybe on some frequency I picked up something from her that made me wary. Anyway, football seems to put you out there for girls, and sometimes you pay more attention to your dick than your brain.

After the fight with Aidan, she ran up to me with ice and a first-aid kit. She cleaned my face and bandaged my jaw, hovering over me. No one else was around. No one else seemed to care, and I felt like crap. When it was time to leave, she told me about the party.

"Come out with me, we'll have fun," she said. "Don't go home alone and feel sorry for yourself." She smiled and looked into my eyes. "I'll take care of you."

I didn't feel like going home anyway, and I wanted to be with someone. Getting the crap kicked out of you does that, and she was hot enough, so why not?

We got on my bike, and if I had any doubts about where things were going, they disappeared as soon as she wrapped herself around me. Beers, an empty upstairs bedroom, and by the end of the party, I was her new boyfriend. We were this power couple to her. It was easier to go along with it than not, which says something about where my head was.

I couldn't claim to be a victim. I got what I wanted too. But there's a big difference between sex and love, and I was definitely in it for the former. Lexie didn't see the divide though. She wanted to do the boyfriend-girlfriend thing 24/7. If I even talked to other girls she had jealous fits that led to make-up sex, even in school. I should have drawn the line at the locker room.

That was a mistake that I paid for. One of many.

I keep walking in the dark. The kitchen. Food, water. Staying alive, that's my focus. If there was other food stored away somewhere, I hadn't found it yet. When the damn hurricane ends, it's not like we can fling open the doors and run free. The outside is already a disaster area. Power lines will be on the ground, floodwater and filth everywhere. That's if we get out. It might take days before someone finds us, if anyone cares enough to look.

There's power left on my phone, and I use the flashlight sparingly to find the cabinet handles, drawers, and the refrigerator. I find sliced cheese and crackers and head back to the gym.

"Eat," I say, putting it in front of her.

"Do you think we'll see our parents or our friends again?"

146

Friends? What are those? "Just eat."

"Why are you so mad at me?"

I stare back at her and don't answer.

JILLIAN

Why is he like that? What did I do? It gets later, but neither of us turns to go to sleep. I'm too wired to close my eyes.

"Do you think the showers work—the ones in the locker room?"

He gets to his feet. "One way to find out."

We make our way to the girls' locker room. No memories there for him. I go into a shower stall and try the water. "They're working," I yell out. I never imagined the thought of showering would make me ecstatic. There are half a dozen shower stalls, and River goes into another one. "Hell, yes!" he yells, as the water pours down.

The cold water makes me feel alive again. There's even soap in the dispensers, so I wash my hair and then my clothes, putting them on soaking wet.

Showering, eating, sleeping, surviving. Life is stripped down to the essentials now.

"Man," River says, coming out of the shower stall, his T-shirt bandages soaking, his wet hair glistening. "I feel human again." He steps closer, and I reach out and touch his shoulder.

"How does it feel now?"

He steps back. "Doesn't matter...you still hungry?"

Denial. That's one way to cope. I nod.

"Me too. Let's go back to the kitchen. A thousand kids go here, there has to be stuff we missed."

We search together this time, but it's hard to tell what's there in the dark. The refrigerator is getting warm. We use our noses like dogs to sniff out what's inside containers. Milk that's turning bad. Cartons of cottage cheese that still smell OK. There's a storage closet, but it's locked. We grab what we can and walk down the dark corridor, devouring crackers like they're prime ribs and scooping out cottage cheese with plastic spoons.

My eyes dart across the room when I hear a scratching sound and make out movement. "Looks like we have company," I say. River flicks on his flashlight and swivels around suddenly.

A mouse scampers across a shelf on the wall. He laughs, relieved, shaking his head. "Let's go into the principal's office. There's a couch in there."

"It's probably locked."

"The lock was broken," River says. "I bet it still is."

He's right. We step through the doorway and I stop. There's a light on over the principal's desk. How can that be? I step closer and realize it's a battery-operated picture light over a poster.

"Any fact facing us is not as important as our attitude toward it, for that determines our success or failure." Norman Vincent Peale

I plunk down on one side of the couch and River stretches out on the other, leaning his head back on the cushion.

"Can I tell you something?"

"What?" he says, guardedly.

"When you were…away, I…missed you."

I'm not sure how to go on. He wasn't a boyfriend or even really a close friend, but still…I liked knowing he was next door, that I'd run into him. I felt a connection, aside from being neighbors. He was easygoing and fun to be around. Before, anyway.

He looks back at me, and for the briefest moment he becomes the River with the pale green flirty eyes and the private smile again. Then his face hardens.

"Then you were the only one who did."

"What about your dad?"

"He didn't lose sleep over it."

"How can you say that?"

He shifts and throws a leg over the back of the couch. "Aside from his job, football was his life, like everyone in this place. When I didn't play anymore, I didn't exist."

RIVER

I shouldn't have started. But once I start I can't shut up. Talking doesn't change anything, but something about the way she's listening...

"There was so much I hated about football," I say, putting it into words for the first time. "The endless practice, the expectations, to fight, to do better, never to coast, the vise that the game puts on your life. And the bullshit cheering from everyone like you were some kind of..."

"God?" she asked.

"Yeah, until you weren't, a game later or a week later, or whenever you screwed up and lost or broke your neck. But you know what the worst was?"

"What?"

"Having a coach who thought he had to rip you to shreds before he could build you up."

"What do you mean?"

"Sports are supposed to build character and teach you about camaraderie, right? But the Briggs way was to shove your face into the ground and make you eat dirt until you manned up and played better. To him, it's a blood sport about winning, no matter the cost."

"If you could start all over again, what else would you do? What else was important to you?"

"I used to fantasize about doing nothing, total inertia. How pathetic is that? Do you know how it feels never to have time to yourself? To have every minute of your day planned out for you, with no time to just screw around and have fun? With barely enough time to sleep? In my other school I was in the drama club."

"I remember."

"My mom was an actress before she met my dad. She kept scripts at home for the movies she tried out for. She was starting to become successful, but then she gave it all up."

"Why?"

"My dad convinced her it was more important to stay home with me, plus he wanted her there for him when he got home—dinner waiting and all that crap—"

She rolls her eyes.

"That's probably why she got cancer. He gave it to her." I punch the cushion with my fist. I'm shaking again. I reach for a pill. I'm out. Shit, I forgot. I open the bottle and lick the inside for any powder left, something, anything. She looks at me in shock, pity, whatever, but I don't care. I start to throw the bottle across the room, and then stop. Not with my name on it.

If I was never born, she could have had the life she wanted.

"Why didn't you make time to join drama?"

"Briggs wouldn't hear of it."

"Why was it up to him?"

"Why talk about it now?" I ask. "It's over." She reaches for my hand, but I pull back. "I'm not the same person I was two years ago."

"Everyone changes."

"You don't understand. No one does."

There's a crash outside, then another like the building is getting slammed by a battering ram. What's next, the roof over our heads?

"Let me look." I start to get up.

"Stay River, please."

Things die down, at least for the next few minutes, and I sit back.

"You know what I read?" Jillian says.

"What?"

"You can't find peace by avoiding life."

"I'm not looking for peace," I say. *Maybe justice.* "I'm looking to be left alone."

CHAPTER 20

JILLIAN

There's a loud banging outside. "River...what—"

"Quiet," he says, his face close to mine. He gets up and pulls the knife out of his back pocket. I sit up, fear spreading through me.

"Where are you going?"

"I saw a light somewhere," he says.

"It was lightning, what else?"

"Go into the girls' room. Don't leave until I come for you."

"Why?"

"I want to look around."

"Who could it be?"

He shrugs.

"Briggs?"

"I hope not."

"So what if he sees you?"

"He has an order of protection against me, OK?"

So it was true. "Why?"

He doesn't answer.

I enter the dark, airless bathroom. It smells of disinfectant. The black-and-white penny-tile floor is damp and slippery. The steel door slams, and I press my ear against it, which makes no sense.

I don't know much about Briggs, but I remember when Chris Jones, one of the players, told us about the time Briggs took the team out for steak dinners.

"He let us order one-pound rib eyes, double lobsters, anything we wanted," he said. "As a joke, Clint Hagel asked Briggs if he could order a filet mignon to take home for his dog, and Briggs said yes! He promised us another steak dinner in three months, any restaurant we picked, if we kept it going."

Coach Briggs had worked at top prep schools on the East Coast, but moved to Harrison when our coach retired. He hit the ground running from day one, changing the way the school thought about football.

Hustle, hit, and never quit.

Our blood, our sweat, your tears.

All it takes is all you've got.

We knew the familiar slogans, but Briggs's mantra was short and concise: "We play to win." Since he started, more than half of the players had been on track for full scholarships to top schools.

The principal wanted a story on Briggs, so I remember stopping River in the corridor one day to get a quote from him.

"Red," he said, tugging at my ponytail. He was flirty with everyone. I knew better than to take it personally.

"I prefer, 'Jillian,' actually," I said, leaning away.

"OK, Jillian Actually," he said, straight-faced. "What can I do you for?"

154

Do me for? I tried to stifle a smile. "Seriously, I'm writing a story on Coach Briggs. What do you think of him?" The smile faded as he glanced away, lost in thought for a moment.

"He's in a 'league of his own,'" he said, making quote marks with his fingers.

"Want to expand on that?"

He shook his head and walked off.

Another player agreed. "There's no one like Briggs. His whole world is football." He paused, "Only there's too much practice." I jotted down what he said and started walking to class, but he caught up to me. "Whatever you do, don't use my name."

"Why?"

"He'll freak."

I did name the dad of a player who emailed the school paper after his son left the team due to a knee injury.

"Practice should be limited to no more than two-and-a-half hours a day and twelve-and-a-half hours per week with time off during the summer," he said. "The demands a coach makes have to be realistic."

Briggs's response?

"Our ranking speaks for itself."

The principal was more effusive. "It's an honor and privilege to play for our team," he said. "No one is forced to. It takes time and commitment. If a player feels the demands are excessive, he's free to step down at any time. I don't think I have to remind anyone that for the first time we're heading toward the finals, and we couldn't be prouder."

Why were the players so nervous talking about Briggs? Why did Briggs need protection against River? I had heard of orders of protection, but I thought they were for violent boyfriends or husbands. I'd never heard about River getting in trouble, except for the fight with Aidan. Did he threaten Briggs? Fight with him? That would be crazy and hard to

155

imagine. But as Kelly said, maybe he snapped. Maybe the pressure got to be too much for him.

I try to think of what else happened before he left. The only thing I can think of is the fire. Kids talked about it, but it wasn't suspicious. It started in Briggs's office, just before River was sent away. Aside from the smell of smoke, the only damage was to some filing cabinets and the walls around them. It was probably electrical, someone said, because workers had been fixing the lights.

Did River start it? Why would he jeopardize everything to vandalize Briggs's office? We lived next door to each other. I saw him in school and with other people. I trusted him. He wasn't crazy. He didn't seem dangerous.

At least before.

But maybe that was all me. I was needy. That happens when your dad is there one day and gone the next. You never recover from losing a parent.

It was just a kiss.

Kelly once talked about how guys were different from girls.

"Kissing doesn't mean the same thing to them. To guys it's more about what comes next. It's less emotional, especially if you hardly know the guy."

That struck me as something my grandmother might say. But I didn't tell Kelly that.

Was I crazy to trust River now? He had meant it when he slapped me—I'd seen it in his eyes. Prison changed him. Awful things happened there, everyone knew that. Maybe now he was a totally different person than the one I thought I knew.

Suddenly my whole world seems filled with questions, not answers. Am I more afraid to be inside the bathroom or out? Who would be crazy enough to come here, besides us? I ease open the door and make my way along the dark corridor, my hands reading walls, doors, cabinets, and indentations. If Briggs is here, he'd probably be in his office.

I make my way. English, the science room, another door to the boys' bathroom, the guidance counselor's office, and finally Briggs's office. I walk along silently. I stop just before the office door. The glass window in the door is dark. As I take a step closer, an arm snakes out of nowhere.

"No," I scream as a hand clamps down forcefully over my mouth, pulling me against a hard body.

CHAPTER 21

JILLIAN

I work to break free, but I'm held in place, a strong arm around my neck. I try to open my mouth, to bite the hand, but I can't move.

"I told you to stay in the bathroom," River hisses. My heart is drumming against my chest. Finally, he releases me.

"God, River, what's wrong with you? You nearly scared me to death! I thought I'd help, if—"

"—No, you'd get in the way!"

"I couldn't stay in the—"

"—Let's go back," he says. "It was probably lightning or...or I'm just..."

Now he's losing it?

Then we see it at the same moment. A light—outside somewhere.

"I'm going out," he says. "I have to find out."

"Are you crazy?"

"Yeah, that's the problem." He rushes toward the door.

"River! You'll get killed, don't!"

"Five minutes and I'll be back."

There's a thick tree limb outside, and he props it between the door and the jam.

"Stay here," he says.

"I'm coming with you."

"Don't!"

I reach for him, but he slips past me.

I go running after him until a gust throws me back against the wall, slamming my arm. I manage to get to my feet. River hunkers down near the building looking everywhere, but there's no flash of light now, nothing. The only movements are random objects somersaulting in the wind. The rain is hitting like daggers against me. River shields his face with his arm.

"Whatever it was is gone. Come back inside!"

"I want to circle to the other side," he says, edging past me, close to the building. There's a powerful gust and then it dies down. A tree branch the length of a Chevy comes slamming down a few inches in front of us.

"Christ!" River yells, jumping back just in time.

"Can't you see that's a warning? There's nothing out here, River! We have to go back inside." I grab his arm and pull him back toward the door. "Listen to me, now!"

He crouches down and looks around one more time.

"River!" I scream. "There's no more time!" The wind starts up again, and I reach back and grab onto the door handle to brace myself. But River pulls away and walks ahead until a wind gust slams him into the building.

"Ow," he shouts, falling to the ground. He's breathing hard, obviously shaken. I run to him and pull him up and toward the door.

We're about to go inside when there's a flash of light in the distance—the headlights of a car. But the downpour is so heavy, it's impossible to tell whether it's coming closer or driving away. River's face looks haunted, scared, his eyes fixed on the lights until the car turns and the red taillights dim, finally disappearing into the distance.

We slam the door behind us, sinking against the wall, catching our breath. "You have to tell me what's going on, River. You almost got us killed out there. Is that what you want? None of this makes sense to me. You have to talk to me. I can't stand it."

"It doesn't make any difference."

"How can you say that?"

"Knowing's not going to change anything."

"If someone was here…what am I supposed to do or feel if I don't know what the hell is going on?" There's a long silence.

"C'mon," he says. I follow him to Briggs's office. He stops and tries the door. Locked. He digs a key from his pocket and unlocks it, hesitating in the doorway, as if he's expecting Briggs to jump out of a secret hiding place. I follow him in, and he looks around like he's seeing it for the first time. "It's a long story," he says, finally.

"We're not going anywhere. We have all night."

RIVER

I spit on Briggs chair, then kick it over and kick it again. It smacks against the wall and ricochets. My heart's in overdrive. Where the hell to start?

The window frames shake so hard my bones vibrate, like I'm inside the spin cycle of some monster washing machine.

"You know anything about a juvie prison?"

She shakes her head.

"It's a hellhole, ten times over. They treat you like a deranged animal they have to lock in a cage. If you don't do what they want, the guards

161

beat you, or just walk out and let the other guys do it. Then they drag you to the shrink who screws you up even more with pills."

"What kind of pills?"

"Psych pills—pills to make you lose your mind, so strong you're comatose and they don't have to deal with your shit. Pills that they hope will stop your heart so they can bury you."

"Why did you take them?"

"Why? Because if I didn't they'd lock me in solitary until I 'changed my mind.' Or one of them would hold me down while the other would force my jaws open and shove them down my throat."

She looks shocked, disgusted. This is so not her world. It wasn't mine either, but now it is. It'll be part of me for the rest of my life.

"It has nothing to do with you being sick or having anything wrong with you, even though everyone has something wrong with them after they're inside, even if they didn't come in that way."

Jillian looks at me, uncertain.

"What the pills do is draw a curtain down between you and reality." I'm realizing it for the first time, now that I'm saying it out loud. "They don't care what effect they have on you. All the guards know is if you're stoned out of your mind you'll be quiet instead of screaming at them or beating up on somebody, and if you happen to freak and go psycho on them, then they're within their rights—or they think they are—to tie you down in an empty room for an eternity so that you can't even get up to take a piss.

"The food is rancid. The place is filthy. Toilets are backed up and sometimes we didn't shower for days or even get toothpaste." I shake my head. "I fought them at first, fought the pills, fought whatever there was to fight, from the roaches to the spoiled, shit food. I'd lie on my ratty sweat-soaked cot watching bugs crawl up the walls and feeling hot, cold, nearly unconscious, my heart racing, laughing, crying, sick to my stomach puking, eyes seeing, eyes blind, crazy sounds, silence as wide as death, flashing lights, everything, nothing, fantasies so deep and dark I forgot who I was and whether I was alive, dead, or somewhere in between…and all the time I remembered just one thing, how I hated Briggs, how I hated his guts so badly I wanted to kill him."

I watch her face and say, "You know enough now?"

"God…" She covers her mouth and struggles to take in a breath.

"After a while it was just too hard to keep fighting. I half wanted to die anyway, so I took the pills, even though little by little they destroyed part of my brain, which obviously was the intention of the bogus shrink. If you OD'd, there was one less sorry son-of-a-bitch kid to deal with. What did they care what the body count was? They were getting paid either way, pretending what they did for a living was justifiable. Anyway, they were convinced that we deserved to be there because we were the scum of the earth and a threat to society. And you know what else?"

"What?"

"The more inmates they got, the more money they made since it was privately run, not government. So kids who didn't do anything—kids who jaywalked or threw a cigarette butt out a car window—got picked up and put before a judge who was being paid off by the prisons."

"Did your dad know anything, didn't he come to see you?"

"It was a ten-hour drive and he had work, so he visited me every couple of weeks. He saw some of what was going on. He's pretty smart. But it was easier to pretend he didn't…"

"Why didn't you tell him what it was like?"

"You don't think I tried?" I ask. "But it was so off the charts he thought I was making it up so he'd feel sorry for me."

Talking about that place, it all starts to come back to me. "The visiting area wasn't like the rest of the hellhole. It was cleaned up to throw visitors off. And they didn't let outsiders go to our rooms."

"Why not?"

"Something about disturbing the privacy of the kids, like we had rights. Anyway, my dad is good at deceiving himself. He was a marine."

"But he must have known something—"

"What he knew was I had destroyed the perfect life he had made for me. All he saw was I tried to quit the team and I was thrown out of school—never mind why—and lost my chance at a scholarship, and no one wanted to touch me anymore. So he figured I deserved what I got and I had to man up and take the punishment."

I'm shaking all over, sweating harder now, only it's a cold, sick sweat.

"I think when he went to bed at night he probably woke up with nightmares about what my mom would have said if she knew where I was and he was letting it happen. That probably drove him out of his mind—knowing how it would have destroyed her."

The words spill out in a rush. "The heat was like this. Only worse. There was no air-conditioning, or at least they never turned it on because they didn't think we deserved to breathe. The bed smelled, and if they didn't like the way you looked at them, they beat the shit out of you and didn't let you shower."

"River, I'm so—" her voice quavers.

"—So that's where I went. That's where they sent me. The MVP. To be rehabilitated—all because of Briggs."

"Rehabilitated?"

"That's the bullshit they feed the public. They're supposed to purge you of whatever they stuck you in there for."

She reaches to take my shaking hand. I pull back.

"Was there school? Aren't they supposed to continue your education?"

"The classes were for morons. I usually fell asleep, but that wasn't allowed either."

"River...I'm so sorry...I know that doesn't make sense now...but I am. I wish I had known. I would have done anything to help you."

164

"No one could have done anything."

"I don't believe that."

I study her face and turn away.

"I can't believe your dad couldn't have done something to get you out of there."

"My dad's face told me everything I had to know. Disappointment. He just blamed me for ruining the fantasy world he lived in that would raise him up after a crap day at work and a house without a wife."

"But you got out—how?"

"One night when he was probably on his fourth scotch, the guilt must have hit him so hard he couldn't stand it anymore because the next morning he hired the best lawyer in Texas. They got me out in like an hour, probably by scaring the shit out of the warden. His timing was impeccable. I left two days before the kid in the next room hanged himself with the rope they used to whip him, and a state investigation broke out. It was all over the newspapers."

I lean toward her, grabbing her wrist. "Paying judges for each kid they sent away. How's that for justice and the American way?"

"I saw that on TV."

"If my dad expected me to feel indebted to him, he was wrong."

JILLIAN

I'm sick inside. My mom gets paid to ask questions when things don't look right. She taught me to do that. So how did we miss something so wrong under our noses? Things were hushed up after he left. Nothing made it into the papers. But being sorry won't help River now. I go in a different direction.

"What was your mom like?"

"There for me."

Despair. I've never heard that in his voice before. "But your dad always came to the games." I sit. "He seemed so proud of you."

165

"On the field, the only place my dad could relate. That was the reason I started to play. My dad took every win as one for himself too. Other kids could get knocked down, break bones, but not me." He shakes his head. "This is boring shit. I don't even know why I'm telling you."

"It's not boring, River." I need to keep him talking to me.

The building rumbles around us, trembling like it's scared, then it stops.

"Jesus," River says.

"Keep going," I say. River gives me a look of annoyance. This is hard for him to talk about. "You can't give up. Your life isn't over."

"Right...I'm still breathing..." He shakes his head. "You can't know. No one ever tied your hands and held you in a choke hold."

"Fight back. It's not too late. You can't keep this inside you. It's eating you up."

"I don't *care* anymore."

"I know you do." Anger surges through me. I hate the way he's letting everything that happened beat him down and destroy him. That's not who he is.

He starts to answer, then stops when we hear an earth-shaking boom followed by a creaking groan. River charges down the hallway toward the stairwell.

CHAPTER 22

RIVER

"What do you think that was?" Jillian screams, coming toward me.

"The roof," I shout. I stop short, and she crashes into me, slamming my bad shoulder. I nearly double over from the pain.

"Ow!"

"River, omigod, I'm so sorry, are you OK?"

I squeeze my eyes shut and try to breathe. I grab the doorknob to brace myself, and we huddle against the stairwell door as the building tremors beneath us. It's like a crazy sick theme-park ride. I force myself to push the door open.

"Don't, River!"

I shake free and bolt up the staircase, and she runs behind me. As we get to the third floor, there's a thunderous groan, and the building seems to recoil from the blow. We both grab the handrail to steady ourselves. Finally, I pull open the stairwell door.

We both stop.

A crack several feet long runs along the corridor ceiling. I can see the light of the sky through it.

"A tree…it must have crashed on the roof. What else could have done that?" she says.

It's hard to imagine wind strong enough. Water is cascading through the gaping hole. Unless the rain stops the upper floor will be flooded in minutes—if the roof doesn't collapse altogether. I grab her arm, and we run back through the door and down the stairwell to the first floor.

"What do we do when the water starts rushing down here?"

"We're safe for now," I say, but I'm not sure I believe it. "The rain will stop, it has to."

We end up back in the principal's office where it's quieter, slamming the door behind us.

"Let's get some sleep now," I say. Better than talking and going over everything. I give her the couch and get into a chair. "Who knows what the hell is ahead."

"You had a dream," she blurts out.

"What?"

"A nightmare, in your sleep."

"What did I say?"

"You didn't talk much, but you sat up and then reached for your knife."

How much did she find out? "A kid in the place…had throwing knives. I learned to use them."

"How did he get them?"

"Somebody brought them in for him. I don't even think the metal detector worked. He hid them inside a broken wall. They never found out."

"He let you use them?"

"Between the guards' shifts we used to sneak into the rec room." I feel like heaving when I think of that place. "It had a Ping-Pong table but no paddles, and a target, but no darts. So we used to throw the knives. I got pretty good."

"What happened, River? Why did they arrest you?"

I look at her and turn away. "A lot of stuff. Starting with the drugs."

"What drugs?"

"You don't know?"

"I heard a rumor, that's all."

Hard to make out if she's playing me or not. "Somebody planted coke in my locker. I thought everybody knew that."

"I heard that but I didn't believe it, and I couldn't find out anything. And you were still in school."

I look at her skeptically.

"I'm telling you the truth," she says. "When did it happen?"

"A couple of weeks before everything blew up."

JILLIAN

My mind flashes back to a gossip blog that lasted until the principal heard about it. It was called *ISpy*. I read it and then forgot about it. Half of it sounded made up anyway.

Under hot tips, someone wrote anonymously: *Vindictive b*t*h? How far would a jilted team player go for revenge?* I was with Aidan when I read it.

"Who do you think the vindictive bitch is?"

"Could only be one person."

"Who?" I asked.

"Lexie."

"How do you know?"

"She got dumped," he said.

"By River?"

"Who else?" he said.

"What did she do for revenge?"

"I heard rumors, that's all."

"About what?" I said.

He holds his thumb on one nostril and inhales. "Someone put coke in his locker."

"Why?"

"To get back at him."

"How did you know about the coke?"

"You think I got the drugs for her?" Aidan said. "I'm not crazy."

Aidan wouldn't do anything that would jeopardize basketball. I was being crazy. But he worked in the gym office. Did he find River's combination or tell Lexie where to look? Or maybe he just looked away when he saw her looking in the file drawer she had no business looking in.

She had to know River would get expelled if the school found drugs on him. That went a lot further than getting back at someone who broke up with you. But that was the last I heard of it. And River was still in school.

I turn back to River. "Who planted the coke, do you know?"

"Maybe."

"What happened?"

"It was there one day, I don't know how," River said. "I didn't think anyone knew my combination."

"Did you report it?"

"I didn't have a chance. Briggs told me. Someone sent him an anonymous note."

"What did he do?"

"He said he knew it was bullshit and that I wasn't a cokehead. He said he'd hold the coke for evidence, in case the person tried something else."

"So you don't know why they did it or how?"

River smirks and lifts his hand as if there's no point in going on.

"What happened, after that?"

"A lot, Jillian."

"I...I don't understand."

"Lexie and I had a thing for a while."

"I know. So?"

He shrugs. "I'm a guy, she came on to me heavy, so I fooled around with her. It was nothing serious, but she wouldn't stop. She thought we were this power couple."

I look at him, not understanding.

"Have you seen the colored bracelets on her ankle?"

"Yeah."

"Each one is for one of her..."

"What?"

"Conquests," he says. "But I was the star player...she couldn't go any higher. " He shrugs. "She was insecure—that meant a lot to her, and she wouldn't let go. But something happened," River says. "I got into deep shit with the coach, and I finally used that as an excuse and broke up with her."

"What happened?"

He coughs and looks away. "He caught us in the locker room—one night, after practice. She sneaked in after everybody had left. I didn't even know she was planning to, but she liked to take chances and get over on people. Danger turned her on. Anyway, it was dark, and we were in the back. I told her it was stupid to be there. That we should go out somewhere. But she wouldn't listen. Finally, I gave in. I thought we were alone, only we weren't."

"What do you mean?"

"Briggs walked in on us. He's a goddamn bloodhound."

171

"What did he do?"

"He grabbed her by the back of the neck and without a word he forced her out the door, slamming it behind her. Then he walked back to me and said, 'Down on the floor.' He made me do fifty push-ups—with his boot on my back."

"Why didn't you report him?"

"Report him? Who do you think they'd believe? I wasn't exactly the model student. Plus he had the coke too, so there were two strikes against me if he wanted to get me tossed." He shakes his head. "It gets more complicated."

CHAPTER 23

RIVER

I started to get strange vibes around Lexie. It was like being on a slow-moving train that without warning races out of control and can't be slowed down. She got hold of me and the closer she got, the more I realized I couldn't get free. Like that weird old movie *Fatal Attraction*. A one-night thing turns out to be the start of something that grows sicker and sicker until you realize the girl is a complete nutso, but by then she's got you by the balls.

The first inkling I got of what she was really like was after cheerleading practice one afternoon. She was bitching about one of the new girls who joined the team. She seemed obsessed with her. The girl wouldn't listen to Lexie; she had her own ideas and wouldn't cooperate. With Lexie, it was her way or the highway. They were doing this pyramid, she said, and "what ended up happening" was that the girl got thrown forward. She landed hard and broke her ankle, and that was it: she was off the squad. She was lucky she didn't break her neck. She was thrown from eleven feet in the air to the hard ground. Lexie didn't know why they didn't use mats or padding.

"Wasn't there a spotter?" I asked.

"She was in the bathroom; she took a break."

The whole thing hit me wrong. Just the way she told me. It didn't faze her. She saw it as karmic justice or something.

"Who was holding her?" I asked.

"I had one leg," she said. Before I could say anything she said, "She fell! It wasn't my fault. She shouldn't even have been part of the pyramid. She didn't know what she was doing."

"How did she fall?"

"She leaned forward, she lost balance, she was an amateur—how should I know? I warned her. I told her she wasn't ready for the squad."

We were in my room watching TV. I started to turn away.

"Let's not fight," she said. In seconds she was on top of me and that kind of ended the conversation. When I thought about it later, it was clear.

Lexie set it up. She wanted her to fall.

A flash of light from outside hits the window again. Then it's gone. Jillian's eyes widen. I get up.

"River, don't!"

"Stay here." I crack open the office door and take a step out into the hallway, the water pooling around me. I look around. Nothing. A smashing sound from outside makes me jerk back. Then I charge down the hall.

JILLIAN

River's run off somewhere again, crazed, frantic. I'm alone. The window frames whine incessantly in the wind. Rain pelts the building in an unrelenting torrent. I go out to the hall. The entire first floor is flooded now. I rush through the pooling water to the stairwell and see water rushing down the stairs.

Stop it, stop it, I want to scream. Everything is out of control. Like a two-year-old, I want my mom. Only I have no idea where she and Ethan are now. Hours ago she was on the radio, but then she disappeared into a sea of static. Is she alive? Is she out in the storm reporting? Marooned somewhere? Did Ethan reach Austin? What about Kelly and Aidan, and River's dad? No TV, net, phone, or radio.

Where is my world? Everything inside me seizes up, my heart skipping, beating soft and then hard, like it's lost its normal rhythm.

Then random thoughts of things that could happen. The bizarre stories you hear about after a hurricane: people disappearing after torrents of water shoved them off embankments, others who had heart attacks and died from stress.

Or the eerie, inexplicable stories like the one in the news about a man who had left a stack of folded laundry on his bed. When he returned home after the storm, the whole house was flooded, everything he owned waterlogged and destroyed. His queen-size bed was floating like a boat in the water. But on top of it was his laundry, exactly as he had left it. Neatly folded. Perfectly dry.

I stand in the corridor trying to hear something, but how can I with the storm insulating us from any other sounds. I see a dark shadow and jump.

"Nothing," River says, appearing out of nowhere. He hesitates. "But…"

"But what?"

He bites at his lip.

"Tell me."

"I have this feeling."

"What kind of…feeling?"

He runs his hand through his hair. "I don't know." He looks around. "We're getting flooded out here. We have to move."

"Back to the storage closet? At least it has no windows. And upstairs, we're too close to the roof if it collapses."

"Whatever," he says. He's holding back. He looks nervous, uneasy, but trying not to let it show.

"What?" I say.

"Nothing."

We make our way from the office along the corridor. The water's up to our knees now. River opens the closet door with the key.

"How did you get a key?"

"Al."

"Who?"

"The custodian."

"Is he a football fan?"

"An alcoholic," River says. "All it took was a six-pack."

No wonder the flag was still flying. And the water was left on. Then it hits me why he didn't want to come back here. Lexie. I could have sworn that I smelled her perfume in here. I knew the scent. It was strong, musky, and cloying. It was made by Dior. It was called Poison.

CHAPTER 24

RIVER

We pile up the mats and manage to stay dry, almost a foot above the water pooling on the floor. It's better than upstairs with the rain pouring through the roof. I kick aside a roll of paper towels floating in the water. It's claustrophobic in here, like being inside a stuck elevator.

Sure, I think of Lexie. That's why I didn't want to come in here. Once or twice a week we met here during school. It was a goof at first. But then it wasn't. If I didn't want to meet her, she got mad.

"I thought you loved me," she'd say, her eyes darkening. After that, I never knew what she would pull.

Once when we were on my bike, she grabbed my arm so hard that I nearly crashed into the car in the next lane. I freaked. I dropped her at home and rode off without a word. She came over the next day with an expensive speaker system she bought for me. I didn't want to take it.

"I'll never do anything like that again, I swear," she said. "I had PMS and I was down because of the Spanish test I nearly failed. I love you," she said. "I'd never hurt you, you know that, right, River?" She had a way of turning wide-eyed and earnest when it was convenient.

I didn't love her, not even close. I never told her I did, so I don't know why she thought it. I knew it was only a matter of time until she did something worse. *Break up with her*, I kept telling myself, *get it over with*. Only I was afraid to.

• • •

"There's something about Briggs that I don't understand," Jillian says, interrupting my thoughts.

"What?"

"He seems so straight and law abiding, but he makes his own rules, like the keys and the hours of practice."

"Rules? He doesn't care about rules. He has one goal in life, to coach the winning team and reward the guys who get him there and crush the ones who go against him."

"Didn't he ever get in trouble?"

"With who?"

"Teachers, the principal, parents? I mean my way or the highway doesn't endear you to people."

"Would your parents complain if you had your pick of scholarships and you became a star? And the principal? We were heading to the finals and the school was eligible for all kinds of grants. Briggs is a goddamned hero to everybody. No one cares how he does it. Everybody takes his shit, no matter what."

"But that's not everything."

"What planet are you on? The game is about winning. No one's going to touch him."

She lies back and doesn't say anything. I press my cheek to the mat and listen to her soft, steady breathing. Strangely, it calms me. I shift, bumping her arm, and then ease away.

"I wonder where your dad is," she says.

"Probably sitting in his car to prove he was right."

"What was he like—when you were little?"

Where do I start?

"I remember him trying to get me out of diapers," I say, finally. "And taking me to the john over and over to train me. 'Grow up,' he kept saying. His way to get someone to do something was to grind them down."

"How did he get along with your mom?"

"She stuck with him. He worked long hours, and my mom brought me up. We would read scripts together, acting out parts, even goofing around sometimes so I was the female lead and she was the male, so I'd be sensitive to characters of the opposite sex—although I didn't get any of that then...You know what?"

"What?"

"I always thought I had such a great mom, I didn't need a dad. I even resented it when he was around. How sad is that?" I reach for my knife. Click, open. Click, closed, again and again in a familiar rhythm.

JILLIAN

"Let's talk about you for a change," River says.

I look at him warily. "What about me?"

"Did you know your dad?"

He's dead, I'm about to say, out of habit. He sort of is. I get a perverse thrill by lying about him. I'm even good at it. Maybe it's in the genes. Anyway, it's partly true. The only thing still alive about life with him are the memories. A soft, "he's dead," short-circuits the conversation when someone asks. They mutter something about being sorry and then drop the subject because it makes them uncomfortable.

Only I can't lie to River, not after he's opened up to me. I want him to know. Especially now.

"One day we were a family and then we weren't." That about sums it up. It was pretty black-and-white, if you took the time to look. Only none of us did. I guess we didn't want to know. It was easier to pretend things would go on the way they were and that when my dad didn't come home until the middle of the night, it wasn't out of the ordinary.

"What do you mean?"

"I guess it had been going on for a while, but Ethan and I were the last ones to know." I start biting at my nail. It's my imagination, I know, but the wind sounds like women screaming outside.

"My dad worked long hours and traveled a lot. He was a journalist too. That's how he met my mom."

"So?"

"So? So my mom was faithful."

"What happened?"

"There was this girl, a new reporter at the paper. He was helping her with her story. Only it didn't end there. He started staying out late...I remember hearing my parents fighting one night, so I went to the door of my room and opened it to listen.

"'I was out with a guy from the copy desk,' my dad said. 'I lost track of time.'

"'Do you think I'm an idiot, Steven?' my mom said. 'I pay the American Express bills, remember? I know where you go when you say you're working late, or around the corner from work having a drink.'

"'What do you do, spy on me, Ellen?' I heard a door slam and then my mom started crying.

"They started fighting more and more," I tell River, who narrows his eyes, caught up in the story. "And then one day it stopped. No arguing, no talking, nothing. They were rarely in the same room together from then on. They were past excuses. Finally he stopped coming home. Nothing was the same after that."

River blows out a breath. "That's hard."

"I saw his girlfriend's picture online. She was blond like a Barbie with this stupid grin on her face. She was young enough to be his daughter, I swear."

"How old were you?"

"Eight when he left. I never saw him again. Eventually he moved halfway across the country and got a job with another paper, we heard. Just left us. Can you imagine?"

"No," he whispers.

"How can a man abandon his family and turn his back on his kids when they need him? No matter how I felt about someone else, I could never do that. Never. Never, never, never, never."

I squeeze my eyes shut, but it doesn't stop the memories. If only there were a delete key in your head to kill out whatever you wanted to erase from your life.

I stare at the level of the water around us, slowly getting higher. How long would it take until we were submerged?

"I remember seeing the suitcases downstairs. 'Where are you going?' I asked him. 'On a trip,' he said. 'When will you be back?' He didn't answer."

My eyes water even now. It never stops.

"He said nothing," I whisper. "Not even a lie. I think it was worse than having a parent die, because then it's final and there's nothing you can do and you eventually move on. But this way, it left an opening, even though that was ridiculous because he was never coming back. But I was just a kid, and kids don't believe in never."

Neither of us says anything for a while. I sit there thinking back on it, and I remember something I never focused on before. The weather.

There was a nor'easter the night my dad left. I remember thinking it was a crazy night to go out if you didn't have to. I always hated thunder, and when I went upstairs I hid under the covers to block out the sound.

My heart starts to hammer. Is that what your brain does—weave your worst memories together into stories? Or nightmares?

"What happened after that?" River asks.

"Ethan ran away...the next day. My mom called him for dinner and he didn't answer, so we went into his room but he wasn't there. We freaked, both of us."

"Why did he run away?"

"To look for him, to bring him back." I rip at my nail, pulling it off so close to the skin it throbs inside. "Two days later the police found him. He was standing on the side of a street downtown hitchhiking. A stupid little kid. He could have been killed or kidnapped. After that, all I knew of my dad were the stories I saw in the newspaper with his byline. I made a point of never reading any of them." I make a face. "You know what I used to do?"

"What?"

"Take a ballpoint pen and poke holes in his stories. I'd stab them again and again with the pen so when I finished you couldn't read a word. I hated him so much. He started over and pretended that Ethan and I didn't exist. No child support, no anything at first. At least until my mom hired a lawyer and went after him."

"Jesus. Deadbeat dad."

"Yeah. So I know what living with one parent is like. It's a job one person can't ace. At least not if you need to feed your kids on one salary and pay rent and you're paying a lawyer to get child support." I shake my head back and forth, lost in the past. "Don't tell."

"I wouldn't—"

"—*I* don't tell," I say, finishing my thought. "I don't tell...anyone. I never have."

He looks at me questioningly.

"But you know the weirdest thing?"

"What?"

"For some crazy reason I still feel like I did something wrong. Like it was my fault in some way that things weren't right in the family."

"Kids always blame themselves," he says.

"But I still do. I think that maybe if I had been different...Am I crazy?"

River shakes his head. "You can't be."

"Why?"

He looks at me with his haunted eyes and his face softens. "Because I've got the monopoly on crazy."

I'm glad he knows about my family. The pain has changed. It's not as deep anymore. I wonder if that's the way it is for my mom too. I never asked her. Now who knew if I'd ever have the chance.

"What about *your* mom?" Definitely need to change the subject. "Did she work after you were born?"

He shifts on the mat and blows out a breath. He sees what I'm doing, but he goes along. "She gave up acting, but she wrote screenplays. I think he was jealous. He didn't fit into her world of movie people. But mostly it was because it took time away from him. When he got promoted he convinced her to give it up. 'I can buy you whatever you want,' he told her." He grunts. "What she wanted was a life of her own. Being Mrs. Harlan Daughtry didn't cut it for her. And then when he started in the oil business, there were dinners she had to go to with him and lunches..."

My mom would hate that kind of life, I think.

"He thought that should have been enough for her," River says, going on like he can't stop. "It was like he was living a hundred years ago. Then one day," he says, lying on his back, eyes closed, "she got sick."

RIVER

Even through the closet walls we hear the explosive sounds. It's like the end of the goddamn world outside. It's so sick and morbid, I know, but I think of her dead, underground. What would happen if she had been buried here? Maybe her coffin would have floated up out of the ground, like she had no real place in the world anymore. No place to rest, ever.

"What happened?" Jillian asks.

I go back to when it started.

"She was in bed when I got home one day. 'I just have to rest, I'll be fine,' she said. Pretty much from that afternoon on, she was in bed more than out of it.

"She went to doctor after doctor. Then she started going to the hospital for treatments. Weeks later, whenever she got out of bed, there would be clumps of hair on her pillow. I didn't understand what that meant. She looked at me with this pitying expression. She knew what was ahead for me and she was powerless to stop it."

How do you deal knowing that you're leaving your kid to grow up without you, with just one parent—the one who doesn't know how to do the job? The one who can't replace you?

I look at Jillian and think of her story. Some parents choose to abandon you. Others are helpless to stop it.

"Everything in my world changed after that," I say. "What did I care about football when my mom was dying? But my dad needed the Friday night lights more than ever."

JILLIAN

The water continues to seep under the door, rising higher on the mats. River has gone quiet. He's not thinking about the storm. At least not the one outside.

184

"But after you moved, you didn't have to keep playing football. Why didn't you stop when you moved here?"

He exhales hard. "As soon as I told my coach in LA that I was moving, he contacted Briggs. He thought he was doing me a favor. Day one Briggs wanted to see me. It was like it was already decided." River pauses. "I'm so sick of going over this," he says. He rolls over.

Minutes go by. I turn toward him. Is he just breathing softly, or is he asleep?

"You still up?"

"Yeah."

"What are you thinking?"

"About the first time I saw you," he says.

"When was that?"

"The day we were moving in."

"I saw you, but I didn't think you saw me," I say.

"I saw you," he insists.

"When?"

"I was helping my dad carry boxes into the house. You were getting something out of your car and glanced over at me, but I was busy trying not to drop a shitload of dishes."

"Not cool."

"Right." He stops.

"What?" I say.

"What what?"

I swallow. "What did you think?"

"I noticed your hair," River says. "And your blouse."

"Why?"

"Your hair was down on your shoulders. It looked red gold glinting in the sun, like you were painted by some French artist like Renoir."

I'm glad he can't see me blushing.

"You were wearing a pale pink blouse and blue shorts," he says. "I thought...you weren't real."

"I remember your first day in school when you got lost and couldn't find the office."

"I hate first days," he says. "You saved me."

"It's funny that we're neighbors."

"Why?"

"I don't know. The boy next door, that kind of thing."

"You had it bad for me," River says.

"What?"

He laughs. "I'm kidding."

Flashback to "before" mode. His easy sense of humor, his guard down. How long before he slips back into his full-body armor? We're in an airless closet with a locked door and a flooded floor. Crazy, but it feels safe here. If only the real world had a safe room. But reality check, unless the storm stops, the building is going to get slammed even worse. And unless Danielle kills us, we'll be forced to climb up somewhere because the first floor will be flooded out.

I turn on my side, narrowing the space between us. River turns, his back to me.

I don't know how I get the nerve to ask. "Remember...the night...of the full-moon picnic?"

"Yeah?"

I hesitate. "You know the kiss thing."

"So?" he says, finally.

"I was just..."

"What?"

"Never mind."

"What?" he insists. "You can't just—"

"OK, whatever. Did you pick me because I just happened to be there, or did you look for me?"

"Why do you want to know?"

"I just wondered."

He exhales. "I had to kiss someone," he says, an edge to his voice. "You were there, OK? It was convenient. I'm sorry."

"Fine, OK, never mind." I turn away, closing my eyes.

"Now you're mad?"

"I'm not mad. Why would I be?"

"You have a boyfriend."

"His name is Aidan. And it's not like you wasted any time finding someone."

"It wasn't exactly like that."

"It sure looked that way."

"Christ, do you *know* her?"

"Know her? No one knows Lexie. She has no friends."

"She had this shitty childhood, so she's needy and hooks onto guys..."

"You must have liked that then, easy conquest." Why is he making me so mad?

He clears his throat and turns away. "No," he says, "I didn't like it."

Liked wasn't a word you'd use in the same sentence as *Lexie*. And ever since it got around that I was the one River kissed before her, she had it in for me.

I remember the school fund-raiser. I went with Aidan. Lexie went with River. Whenever Aidan and River were in the same room you could almost feel the tension. But River was cool that night, especially around me. He even came over to me to suggest a story for the paper on the time commitment you had to make to join a team.

"Why don't you write it?" I said.

He laughed. "No time, that's the point."

187

Lexie whispered something in his ear and pulled him away. Later she followed me into the bathroom. She was waiting at the sink brushing her long, dark hair when I came out. She stopped, her hands on her hips, her red fingernails ready like weapons. She turned to me as I began to wash my hands.

"Don't come on to him," she said, her mouth in a hard line. "He's mine. We're almost engaged."

"Who?"

"You know who," she said, grabbing my upper arm and squeezing it. "Your next-door neighbor."

"Why would I come on to him? I'm seeing Aidan," I said, jerking my arm back, trying to break free of her grip. Only she tightened it.

"Maybe one boyfriend isn't enough for you."

"Your mind works that way, mine doesn't."

"Remember what I said," she said, finally letting go. "Because if you don't, you will pay."

When I got out of school that day, one of my tires was slashed. I never told anyone.

It was so clear now. He saw me first at the picnic so he used the line about the kiss on me, before he got to Lexie. What a laugh it must have been for him to get over on his next-door neighbor. After Aidan found us, River moved on to someone who offered him a lot more than a pathetic kiss. Not that it matters now. Things like me liking him or him liking me don't matter at all when you're stuck in an airless, filthy closet in a building with a smashed-in roof that will probably collapse. Screw feelings and stupid disappointments, because what we have to look forward to is either getting crushed to death if the building crashes down or drowning because we can't escape. Either way, no one will look for us because everyone would assume the school was vacant.

So after a week, maybe more, they'll find our dead, decomposed bodies.

Or they won't.

And all anyone will remember is that there were unanswered questions about the two kids who thought they could get out of a car in the middle of the freeway and survive a hurricane by running directly into it instead of getting the hell away. Two stupid kids who thought they were smarter than everyone else.

CHAPTER 25

JILLIAN

It feels like there's no air left in the closet. It's claustrophobic. And broiling. I sit up and then lie back down. I turn and look at River. He has a reason to be screwed up. He was locked away, awful things happened to him. But me? Why do I obsess over everything? Why do I always end up a victim, a loser? It was stupid to bring up the kiss. I finally knew the truth, and it only made things worse.

We lie next to each other breathing the same air, but in separate universes, captive to Danielle. "River?"

"What?"

"You know what's so strange?

"What?"

"It feels like you and I are the only two people in the world now. We can't reach anyone else. How scary is that?"

"Nothing new to me."

"But this is different. I mean, before everything happened. You didn't feel like that then, did you?"

He turns from one side to the other. "Nothing stays the same."

I sit up and start rubbing my head. I'm getting a migraine. I search in my backpack for the aspirin tin. Half a pill. Why didn't I check before? I swallow it with a sip from my last box of juice. "God, my head is splitting. There's no air in here."

No answer. I lean forward and start to rub it, but it doesn't help.

"C'mere," River says.

"What?"

"Move over, here."

He edges over on his mat, making room for me, and I slide over. He sits up, leaning back on his heels. I move closer and he takes my head in his hands.

"Lie back," he says, lowering my head to the top of his thighs. His fingers slide through my hair and he massages my scalp, making slow, deliberate circles, around and around in a hypnotic rhythm. He tugs gently on my hair, slowly taking it from side to side, and then up and down getting the blood flowing. My scalp tingles, and I sink against him.

"Where did you learn that?"

"You like it?"

I nod. It's all I can do.

He slips a hand under the back of my neck, slowly rubbing the tight muscles, then his touch grows firmer, using strokes that fire every nerve in my body. I exhale, feeling myself sink back against him even more. I can't help it. Then, just as quickly, I want to sit up and take it back. I can't let him know what he's doing to me, how I feel inside, but it's too late. My body won't stay still. A deep ache of longing electrifies me.

He stops.

Neither of us moves. The storm outside seems to have quieted, the raging wind and hammering rain replaced by a wide expanse of eerie silence. The only sounds are the two of us drawing in breaths, or trying to, all the tightness inside me unraveling, turning to need. He winds his fingers into my hair, gripping it tightly, locking me in place. I'm captive, his prisoner. His face is so close I can feel it when he exhales. My lips part. I want to cry out, to call his name.

My heart slams so hard I'm sure he hears it. I stare up at his eyes, remembering his mouth on mine, his lips teasing the skin on my neck, and I wait. Seconds go by. Why is he doing this to me? What does he want?

His fingers loosen abruptly and he exhales, slowly sliding back, separating himself from me. It feels like one of his knives has hit dead center inside my heart.

"Get some sleep," he says, in a hoarse whisper.

No! I want to cry. I was so wrong. He feels nothing for me. He was just being nice for a change, trying to relieve my headache. Or maybe he was just testing virginal me to amuse himself. I move back to my mat and curl up in a fetal position.

RIVER

Something about touching her hair, her neck, the softness of her skin as she was stretched out in front of me. I nearly lost it. Another second and I would have crushed her under me. I would have been all over her and then opened myself up, telling her everything I keep inside me.

But I woke from the dream and caught myself. I remembered who I am. It was my fault to start. I shouldn't have touched her. I can't be that person again. I don't have anything to give anymore. She deserves someone who's in one piece, who doesn't exist on a diet of pills. I double over and try to push everything out of my head, every thought, every urge, the pain of wanting. Pretending she's not near me, pretending that the soft gasps I hear are not the sounds of her crying.

JILLIAN

I should stop, but I can't. I keep replaying it, only this time the tears come. His hands on my scalp. My nakedness to his touch. His fingers in my hair, so gentle at first, then stronger, as if he were taking possession of me.

But that was crazy me. He stopped; he didn't have to. He moved away. He's asleep now, his thoughts on anything but me.

Why didn't I ever see things for what they were? Why did I turn a five-minute scalp massage into a desperate declaration of love that I hoped would end up with him kissing me? I was 180 degrees from reality, no surprise.

I should be thinking about Aidan, anyway. I could only imagine what he'd be thinking if he knew where I was right now.

Then it dawns on me. I never felt this way with Aidan, and I never will. I've been lying to myself all along.

If you love someone at first sight, it usually goes downhill from there, I'd told Kelly. That was laughable, and she knew it.

Aidan is dependable. He wouldn't abandon me. But dependable isn't a synonym for love. And it isn't a substitute. It's just a poor excuse.

I reach for my diary in my back pocket. But it's not there anymore. It must have slipped out somewhere, all my secrets probably drowned in floodwater now. But that's OK. If we make it out of here, I'll start another diary going forward. It will hold the story of after, not before. Life lived outside my head, not in it, because Danielle is changing my thinking about everything. She's like the car coming toward you, going the wrong way on a one-way street. If you survive and live to talk about it, it makes you vow to live differently. In the sun, instead of the shadows. Not hiding in your head.

I think about magazine articles that ask what you would do if you knew you had only twenty-four hours left to live. Daredevil stuff like ice climbing or coasting down a mountain on a luge? Skydiving? Would you forget your fears and go out into the world to explore it, or sit tight at home as the minutes ticked by, popping Xanax and crying to your friends on the phone?

I think about River's mom. I read about other people who went through the same thing. Some actually said they felt thankful because living on the edge elevated every moment of life they had left and changed the way they viewed the world. Trivial annoyances fell away and they rejoiced in every singular waking moment with a new appreciation.

Suddenly I'm obsessed with last chances and saying things while there's still time. What if River was the last person I'd see for the rest of my life?

Or not. It could just be the room. I could be going crazy because we're in a space without enough oxygen.

"I'm going out."

"What?"

"I need air...it's claustrophobic in here."

"Into the storm?" he says, in disbelief.

"The hall, the gym, anywhere." I drop down into two feet of water, and then turn the knob.

"I'll go with you," he says.

The wind is keening again. We slosh through the wading pool of the first floor, silhouetted by the gray light coming in from the classroom windows. We end up in the theater, up on the stage where we're safe from the windows. I turn to him. "Don't be mad at me."

"Mad about what?"

"I...never mind."

"Jesus, why did you start this?"

I don't answer.

"Why would I be mad at you?" he insists. "Tell me."

"Whatever. You know the play you wrote?"

"Yeah?"

"I read it."

"How did you even know about it?"

"I saw it in the drama room and I was curious about it, so after we put out the paper that night, I went back to the room and read it."

"It doesn't matter anyway."

"It's alive, it's real. You're a good writer, River."

His face is blank.

"I mean it. You should keep writing."

"What did you like about it?"

"The honesty."

"You mean the bullshit."

"It's not. You, or the character, Evan, hates all the decisions he's made or that have been made for him. He feels like every day is a compromise, that he's been manipulated by other people for their own needs, and he's seething. You can tell he's uncomfortable in his skin and he wants to change everything, but he's afraid because he thinks it will all blow up in his face."

"Yeah."

"And you know what else?"

"What?"

"Evan was so real I felt like I knew him. I didn't want the play to end."

"I wrote it a long time ago. Everything was different then…more…"

He waves his hand dismissively.

"It must have felt good to write it. To get all of that down."

"Maybe."

"You should keep going, River. Write about the other stuff. Everything you went through."

"Why?"

Why did I write in my diary almost every night? "Because when you get it out you feel better, it frees you."

"What if it doesn't?"

"Then write it for revenge. Tell the world the real story."

"I'll drink to that," he says.

CHAPTER 26

RIVER

I open my eyes, disoriented. I must have nodded off. Something is different. I lift my head. The rain. Did it stop?

Jillian's stretched out next to me on the stage, the outline of her body in shadow. She's awake, looking at me.

"You think it's over?" she says.

"Maybe it just died down for a while."

"Should we look?"

"Not yet."

"What would you do...if this was the last day of our lives?"

I reach for my knife and click it open. "Get back at Briggs."

"For what?"

"Why are we talking about this? You think we're going to die?"

She looks away. The water filling the auditorium is almost as high as the armrests of the seats.

"River?"

"What?"

"Did you ever read *Our Town*?"

"Yeah."

"Do you remember when Emily asks, 'Do any human beings ever realize life while they live it?'"

I close my eyes. I remember reading it with my mom. I can still see her saying the words.

"'Saints' and poets, the stage manager answers," Jillian says, sitting up straight. "I never really thought of that line until now. When everything's normal, you don't take notice of it. You don't see things because you think your life is going to be just the way it is today and the next day and the day after, but it isn't. You have to stop and enjoy it now, while you have it."

"Live in the moment," I say, lacing my words with sarcasm.

"Danielle is a bitch, you were right," she says. "But I learned something from her."

"What?"

"That there's a world outside of mine," she says. "A bigger one."

"And you want to enjoy it, while you have it, right?"

"Well..."

"I don't know whether I want to live or die, so this is one way to find out." I jump to my feet and head for the door.

"River!" she yells. "That's not what I meant!"

CHAPTER 27

JILLIAN

"Come back, River!" I run after him, but he's off the stage and into the water already, wading to the back door of the auditorium, the one with the Exit sign over it. He pulls it open and the wind pushes him back, tearing the door from his grip. "Whoa!" The door slams.

"River!"

He opens it again. "Out into the apocalypse," he yells.

"River!" I scream into the wind. He keeps going and the door slams shut. I yank it open and run after him. The sky is sulfur yellow, and he tilts his face to it. "Hey Danielle! Go home you sadistic bitch."

"River! Come in before she kills you!"

I stare all around me at the carnage. Everything is broken, shredded, slit into ribbons, as if the earth is being beaten back.

"Screw everything!" He's waded out to where the water is waist high and filthy, strewn with garbage. A gust of wind hits him and he sinks back into the waves. I hunker down at the side of the building, afraid to move until the gust dies down. He struggles to get to his feet, pushing aside a garbage can lid and then hurling a lawn chair that's blocking him out of his way.

"River!" I get to my feet and go after him, pushing through the choppy water, but the wind slams me back, and I'm shoved under. I try to catch my footing, but I slip on mud every time I start to get up. I open my eyes under the filthy water and lose my bearings. I need to stand, to get air, but a wall of water surges against me, and I thrash around, gasping for breath. I finally manage to stand, grabbing onto a tree branch to steady myself. I can't get enough air, I can't, I can't. What do I do? *Slow down, you can, just breathe*, a voice inside me says. I look for River, but I don't see him anymore.

"River!"

The wind starts up again, and I see an old tree not far away with a heavy protruding branch. Slowly I make my way over to it and hold on to steady myself. He's here somewhere. Probably just hidden behind something.

"River!" But there's no sound except the whipping of the leaves on the trees. I stare up at the American flag. It's in tatters now, thrashing back and forth, back and forth on the pole, making a loud whipping sound.

"Help!" I don't know how long I can keep myself from getting blown away. There's another tremendous gust, and I lean my slashed cheek against the rough crumbling bark of the tree to block myself from the force. "River!"

I see movement from the corner of my eye. I turn and see him clinging to a tree, breathing hard. "River!" My voice gets lost in the wind. I let go and slowly slosh my way through the water, not sure whether it's better to walk or swim, pushing away roof tiles, rubber pails, siding, and mysterious broken things. "River!"

He looks pained, traumatized. "What happened to you?" I ask.

"Got pulled out," he says, breathless. "I managed to hang onto part of a fence." His face is scraped and bleeding. I try to grab onto him, but the wind starts up again and I get pulled away, like I'm inside a riptide. He lurches toward me, but it's too late. I'm being dragged, like some sadistic person has attached me to the back of a car. My shoulder and back get bumped against bushes and rocks and then I'm thrown under the water, colliding with uprooted trees and dark objects I can't make out. I try to stop myself, but I'm being dragged too fast. There's nothing near me to grip, to hold onto to brace myself.

Then the wind stops. I'm dropped. I slam down hard, ramming my side, filthy brackish water filling my throat. I start coughing and can't stop. I try frantically to steal a breath between coughs, but end up swallowing the noxious sludge and gagging. I try to steady myself by sliding a foot into the crook of a bush. I grasp it to keep myself from getting blown away again.

Just a gust of wind away from death.

Get back inside, a voice inside me says. But I can't. I'm frozen, confused, afraid to move. I don't know where to turn, what to do. What if the next wind gust is stronger? Do I stay put or try to go? Another slap of wind hits me, and I get pushed down again underwater. It's dark. I can't see anything and the only thing I touch is slippery mud below that I sink into. I can hear my heart ready to explode.

Then I'm aware of something above my ankle.

It tightens. It slithers farther up and tightens again, constricting my calf. I reach down and open my eyes underwater.

My stomach lurches.

A snake is coiled around my leg.

CHAPTER 28

RIVER

"Jillian! Jillian!" I call her over and over until my voice is shot. God, Christ, help me.

It's my fault, it's all my fault. I deserve to die ten times over now. I thrash through the stinking water, pushing away a dead cat, tiny birds with open eyes and gaping mouths, heaps of garbage, roof tiles, antennas, satellite dishes.

I should be part of this floating funeral. I deserve it.

The rain punches my arms and back. I'm stranded inside a giant lake, searching, but she's not anywhere. The only movements are the angry wind drifts chopping into the water.

I make my way to the back of the school, my eyes following every movement, everywhere, trying to see into the black water, and up in the trees where tangled electrical wires are wound around the branches in knots and loops like nooses, sending out crackling sparks that ignite like fireflies. What are the chances she's alive? She's got to be, she's got to be, she's got to be. I keep wading, numb to everything else around me.

"Jillian!" I call again and again.

I stop.

"River!"

"Here!" I follow the sound of her voice, running back around to the side of the school, but she's not there. I go the other way, toward the front of the school. She's fifty feet from the front door, head pitched forward, coughing, water coming out of her mouth. I run toward her. A look of panic covers her face. She points to her leg.

I stop.

It's coiled up around her calf like it's taken possession of her. Three feet long. Black with bands of brown. A paler head.

A cottonmouth.

"Is it poisonous?" Her voice breaks. "It is, right? God, River. What do I do? What do I do? Oh my God!"

"Shh." I move closer. "Stay still. Don't move, no matter what." I can't meet her eyes, I can't. Everything inside me seizes up, and I turn away, searching for two tree branches. Trees are everywhere, all around us, but they're old and the arms are thick. There are no smaller pieces I can break off. I step around in the water, searching every broken branch, every dangling arm from the nearby oaks. Something, anything, please. I can't wait. There's no time.

With all my strength I try to rip away at a piece of a tree arm, but it's too thick, it won't come lose. I give up and move on, my heart slamming in my chest.

I glance back at Jillian. She's holding still, almost frozen with fear. Everything inside me tightens. I look away and keep searching. *If she doesn't move, if she holds still, it'll be OK.* I say it again and again in my head. *It won't attack, if it doesn't feel threatened*—at least I think it won't. Why would it? Animals only attack to defend themselves. When they feel threatened. I keep looking, trying to wipe my mind of everything that might slow me down.

There has to be something, anything I can use. And finally I see a thin tree branch dangling down.

That's it.

Two pieces small enough to rip from a nearby tree. I yank hard and they break off. I'm ready. I make my way back through the water to her and I stop. The snake is watching us, as if it knows. I edge closer.

It lifts its head ever so slightly. The tail slowly begins to swish back and forth, back and forth. Almost imperceptibly, it slides higher up her leg, then stops, tightening itself. Imprisoning her.

"No!" she cries, a strangled whisper coming from her throat. She stares down at it, her eyes wide. "River…God, it'll bite you…it'll bite you. Be careful, don't come close, don't!"

I step back. "Sshhh!"

It feels like there's a rock in my throat. I can't swallow. *Stay calm,* a voice in my head says. *Look at the sky, breathe, pray, anything. Hold still. Don't scare it.*

I stand there and wait. Seconds go by, minutes. I don't know how long. I lose sense of time. My head feels heavy, the blood swirling inside of it. I reach out and steady myself by leaning against a nearby tree.

Finally, it settles down. It knows, it has to. It's like it's reading my mind. The round black eyes with the yellow-gold vertical pupils stay open, never blinking, taking in everything around it. I can only imagine the inner sensors the goddamn thing has. Small, probably less than a pound, but smart and deadly. One bite and it's over.

This is survival time. It's you or me. We both know that.

The wind blows harder, pushing me back, like that's some kind of warning from above. I grab onto the arm of a tree and steady myself. I won't let the wind take me again, no matter what. I don't care if it blows 150 goddamn miles an hour. I'm not moving. I'm not letting go.

"God, oh God," Jillian whispers, panting, short of breath, like she's going to pass out from fear.

"Stay calm, Jill, please," I whisper. "Don't move," I say, not sure whether the words are coming out of my mouth or are just in my head.

I move closer.

This is it!

I slip one stick beneath its neck and the other over it, trapping the head tightly with my trembling hands. The head rears up, the mouth opens wide—cottony white inside!

If I had any doubt what it was, it's gone now.

Before it can sink its sharp deadly fangs into my hand, I slash off the head with my knife, using every ounce of strength in my hands.

"Dead!" I shout, dropping the decapitated head onto a rock, relief spilling through me. I untangle the still squirming body from around her leg, and toss it down. "Jesus, it was a cottonmouth!"

"Oh my God!" Jillian screams.

But she's not screaming because I told her. I look down at the decapitated head and it spasms violently, its jaws wide open. It lurches and clamps down on the thing closest to it, a piece of its own headless body. The body jerks up in response, the tail whipping to the side.

Jillian holds still in shock, staring down at it.

"Get back, get away!" I grab her arm, but she stops and grabs the knife away from me.

"Don't!" I try to pull her away but she resists and plunges the knife into the head again and again, until I yank her away.

"I'm not your victim! I'm not your victim," she screams, fury making her whole body go rigid. "I'm not, I won't be," she screams. I try to yank her back, but she won't budge. She stands there defiantly.

y knees up, to turn away from her,

it.

up. I try to turn, to flip her off me,

limp.

ays, breathing hard. Her face chan-

fading away. Her eyes close, momen-

mine, her face so close our lips nearly

tarts to climb off me, embarrassed,

the waist and don't let her move.

," I whisper, pressing my mouth over

p myself. All the emotion, all the need,

r over a year now, explodes inside me.

breathless.

kissing her deeper, my hot skin against

re I want to keep her, our legs tangled,

eft.

My hands cradle his face and then I let

lips on mine, his tongue in rhythm with

carrying me to a place I've never been

hair, pulling at it, pressing myself against

face, his cheeks, his chin, his neck, and his

want to crawl inside him. I've never felt this

er. I don't want this to end. He leans away

g it in his, bringing it up to his lips, kissing

210

don't want to hurt her. I try to draw m

but she won't get off me, grabbing fo

"Stop it," I say. But she won't give

but she hangs on more insistently.

Then suddenly she stops and goe

"I don't know what I'm…" she s

ges, softening, all the determination

tarily. Then she tears up.

Her hips are still pressed against

touch, our hearts pounding. She s

but it's too late. I grab her around

And that's it.

I can't bear it anymore. "God

hers. I kiss her hard, helpless to sto

all the frustration I kept hidden f

"River," she whispers, nearly

I tighten my arms around her

hers, pressing her under me whe

making up for all the lost time.

In case we don't have much

JILLIAN

I didn't expect this. Not now.

go, meeting the pressure of hi

mine, our bodies skin to ski

before. I reach up and grab hi

le   him. I trace the planes of his

m   chest, but it's not enough. I

tha   way about anyone before, ev

and takes my hand, squeezi

each finger, then the inside of my hand and wrist. The feel of his lips on my skin makes me dizzy. He leans away abruptly, pressing his forehead against mine.

"I did look for you," he says, short of breath.

"What?"

"At the picnic, I did look for you. I waited. I wanted to kiss you from the first day I saw you. I finally had an excuse."

I kiss his forehead and his eyes. Tears well up. He's crying, then sobbing.

"Goddamn," he says.

"What is it?"

He looks away, trying to stop, working at blinking back the tears.

"I'm so broken now. I can't be who you want me to."

"Who do you think I want you to be?"

"Normal."

"What's normal?"

"A guy with a brain who has a life ahead of him." He stops, trying to catch his breath. "Not someone who has nightmares and wakes up in a sweat. I'm so messed up now, and I don't know if that will ever change."

"Don't say that. You went through hell, River."

"I'm still there. I want to run away from myself, but I can't. I don't know what to do anymore."

"Just keep kissing me. We'll figure it out."

CHAPTER 29

RIVER

I lose track of time. Her head is against my chest, my arms locked around her. I want to crush her against me. She shifts and I tighten my hold.

"What I wouldn't do for real food. Filet mignon, fries, a wedge with blue cheese dressing, and key lime pie," she says.

"Sshhh."

"Have you ever been this hungry?"

Yes. The memories flow back and everything darkens. Me lying in bed at night, everything inside me aching from being sick and hungry. I exhale, that's all.

"I'm sorry," she says, her expression changing to one of pity, which I don't need. "Let's go back to the kitchen, maybe there's something, anything we missed."

"I looked," I insist.

"Let's look again."

We wade through the water in the dark corridors until we get to the cafeteria, then go through the back to the kitchen. I start opening doors and cabinets, expecting mice or rats to jump out at me. But there are no mice and nothing to eat except jumbo-sized cans of vegetables. I open the refrigerator and slam it shut.

"Wait," she says. She ducks down on her knees in the water, pushing aside containers of warm, spoiled yogurt and cottage cheese. "Yes!" She slides out a brick of American cheese.

"How did I miss that?"

I take my knife and cut open the plastic, then slice a thick piece for her and another one me. "I never thought food could taste this good."

"More," she holds out her hand.

I haven't been this hungry since juvie. My shoulder burns worse than ever and fury rises up in me.

All I can think of is Briggs. I do want to kill him, I wish I had. It's all his fault. Everything is, and I can't live with it destroying me up anymore. I can't live with covering it up.

I focus on Jillian's face, her lips, the way her mouth moves. I'm hungry for her. I wanted her for so long, but I pretended I didn't because it didn't make sense—not when she lived next door to me. But none of that matters anymore. I kiss her again and again and it pushes the memories away, at least for a while.

She eases away slightly. "There's a freezer," she says. "But it's locked."

I lift the lock and study it.

"There's no way," she says.

"No?" I search around the kitchen and find an empty soda can. I stick my knife into it, cutting out a section.

"What are you doing?"

I fold it so it's shaped like the letter M with one pointy end in the middle, then slide the sharp point into the lock and pull it open at the same time. "Done."

"How did you know how to do that?"

"Being locked up was good for a few things." I dig through the freezer once I get it open. "Hamburger, pork loin, chicken."

"Could already be getting wormy," she says.

Just that word. I slam down the lid. I'd rather starve.

We gorge ourselves on cheese and then walk the corridors. It's like being inside a cave with the sound of rushing water and the whoosh of the blowing wind outside.

She's quiet. I know what's coming. It's a girl thing, the way they get when they want to talk about everything. They hit you with a million questions because they can't stand not knowing.

"River..."

"What?"

"You have to tell me."

"Tell you what?"

She looks at me, exasperated. "What happened to you. Why you got thrown out of school. Why they locked you up. I know you want to get it out."

"What I went through for the past year was different than anything you know about."

"Does that change it?"

"Yeah."

"But you're torturing yourself."

"How do you know?"

"Because I knew you before, River."

JILLIAN

What is he thinking? Why did he freak out before?

"River?"

215

"What?"

"At night, while you were sleeping…"

"Yeah?"

"There was so much lightning, the whole gym lit up."

"So?"

I grab his arm. "I saw…your back. The scar."

He squeezes his eyes shut.

"Did you get beaten up in prison? Is that where the scar is from?"

He shakes his head.

"Then how did you get it?"

I hear a sharp intake of breath.

"From Briggs."

"Wait, what? Briggs?"

"Yeah."

"What do you mean?"

"He beat the shit out of me one day…no, actually, two."

My insides seize up. "Why?"

But before he can answer there's a series of explosions, like firecrackers going off in the stairwell.

• • •

Another tree. It must have hit some electrical wires. We see it through one of the windows that miraculously is still unbroken. It's an old tree, probably a hundred years old. It was yanked out by its roots, and it's leaning against the back wall of the building. I don't know how it didn't knock the wall down.

It looks like everything at ground level is airborne. Sacks of garbage, plastic recycling cans, giant grills, lawn chairs, flower pots, wicker chairs, all of it flying like we're watching some crazy kids' movie.

It's got to die down, but when? We go back to the first floor, wading our way through water a foot high. We end up in front of Briggs's office again, I realize.

"What happened?" I try the doorknob. It's open now. River follows me in.

"I tried to quit the team." He goes to a shelf near the window and picks up the football on the floor. "That was what started everything."

"Why?"

"It was sucking up my life."

"Why couldn't you quit?"

"Why? Because Briggs wouldn't hear of it."

"But other players had left."

"Other players weren't me," he says, squeezing the football. "He saw something in me. He invested in me. He thoughts of me as..." He pauses, searching for the right word. "His prodigy or something. Like I was this nonentity who he turned into a star athlete. He really believed he made me. That I belonged to him, and if I wanted to leave I was a traitor. But he was right about something," River says. "Without me, the team didn't have a shot."

"Is that why he beat you up?" He looks up at me, then looks away. "You have to tell me. Now."

He leans up against the wall and crosses his arms over his chest.

• • •

"Practice ended late," he says, staring off, his voice in a monotone. "I was exhausted. It had to be ninety-five out and I was in a sweat, so I decided to shower. I thought everyone had gone home, but after I got into the shower room, I heard voices outside. I waited, not making a sound. Something didn't sound right. Something about the tone of the voices. I was quiet. I didn't turn on the water.

"I leaned close to the wall and knew right away who it was. Ryan and Briggs. Ryan had screwed up that day. He must have been tired because he'd worked so many nights. His parents are divorced. He lives with his sick dad, and they're broke because of the medical bills.

Ryan has to basically support them by doing odd jobs whenever he has free time."

"What happened?"

"Practice was lousy. He was out of it. It was like he wasn't even there because he was so sleep deprived, so he screwed up and Briggs, as usual, took it personally."

I wait.

"You can't tell anyone this, you have to swear."

"I swear."

"Ryan's gay. Not that I care, but Ryan does. He pretends to go out with girls, to like them, but it's bullshit. At night he goes out, he sees different guys, but he doesn't want anyone to know. If his dad found out, he'd go ape shit, so he refuses to come out."

"So?"

"Briggs must have known, because he's probably gay too, and he has a way of playing on everyone's weakness to get what he wants out of them. So he's always picking on Ryan, trying to provoke him."

"Jesus."

"Briggs started yelling at Ryan. He'd gone after him before, but never like this. He was calling him a fucking fairy and a useless faggot and that was just the beginning. I was standing there, and I couldn't believe what I was hearing. Even for Briggs, it was over the top."

I hold my breath.

River stops and shakes his head, as though he's not sure if he wants to go on. Finally he exhales. "He started slamming Ryan against the locker. I heard the metal door shaking from the impact. Ryan was groaning, but he didn't do anything, nothing. It was like he was too friggin' scared to fight back even though Briggs was attacking him. Ryan could have stopped him, or at least tried, but he took it, like he was dead."

"That's so awful."

"A minute later, Ryan started screaming, and that was it. I ran out of the shower room to go help him. Briggs had him down over the bench and he was ripping Ryan's shirt off..."

River stops, his face distorted as it all comes back to him again. Neither one of us says anything. I'm holding my stomach, feeling sick.

"'What the fuck are you doing?' I screamed at Briggs. I threw myself at him, but he's huge, like a wall of muscle, and he came at me, throwing me down. I was on the floor and he started kicking me. When I couldn't get up, he stopped and looked at both of us.

"'Nothing happened,' he said. 'Anyone opens his mouth you'll both lose your scholarships and get thrown out of school. I'll ruin you for life.' That was it. Then he walked out."

"What did Ryan do?"

"He was on the floor sobbing and then he started vomiting, throwing his guts up. 'We have to go to the cops,' I kept saying. 'He can't get away with this.' But Ryan refused.

"'You don't understand,' he said. 'The scholarship is my only way out. If I lose that I have nothing.' He begged me over and over to just forget it, at least for now. He said if it came out he'd kill himself."

"What did you do?"

"I couldn't do anything. He was my friend; I was caught. I felt sorry for him. I had to live with it, but the guilt nearly killed me. I felt like a liar and a traitor, but I had to keep quiet or it would have backfired on him. He got it worse than anyone, so I couldn't say anything. I went home and threw my guts up too. The next day I decided I was quitting the team."

"What did you do?"

"I wrote Briggs an email that night."

"And then what?"

"I sent it that morning. I decided to put it in writing because coming face to face with him wouldn't work. I took the time to get the wording right. I wanted out, only I didn't say it that way. I knew somebody else might see it, so I said I couldn't handle the demands of the team, and that after the upcoming game I was leaving. I knew that he demanded a hundred percent of us and I wasn't able to give that anymore, so it was only fair to drop out so someone else could take my place."

River leans back against the windowsill. He rubs his eyes, and then stares out ahead of him, as if he's reliving it.

"I couldn't tell from the way he acted at practice whether he had gotten the email. It felt weird because he didn't treat me differently than the other guys. We warmed up, we went through some plays, and he acted the way he always did, even though he got pissed at Mark McClane at one point for running over to his backpack to check his phone, so he ripped it out of McClane's hand and threw it across the field. It was the kind of stuff he always pulled, and it didn't surprise any of us. You didn't do things like that around Briggs. He had a hair-trigger temper, and he didn't give two shits about breaking the phone you worked six months to pay for. He took it personally, like you were saying that the rest of your life was more important than being on the field, more important than him."

"Then what?"

"After practice we all went back to the locker room to shower and get our stuff. The other guys were leaving, but Briggs looked at me and told me to wait."

"Where was Ryan?"

"He didn't come in that day. Briggs told him to stay home for a couple of days and get back to himself. A couple of days, can you imagine?

"I was standing by my locker, waiting. Finally all the others guys walked out and we were alone. He walked over behind me and slammed my locker door closed. I turned around and we were face to face. He crossed his arms over his chest and stared at me. He didn't say a word.

"'You got the email?' I finally blurted out. Briggs just stared, not answering, which made me more nervous, so I started talking to fill the silence.

"'It's just a personal thing,' I said, feeling like I had to defend myself, even though he knew I could never be on the team after what he did to Ryan, and then how he went at me. And then Briggs moved in closer.

"'A personal thing?' he said. I nodded. He said, 'You don't join a team and then abandon it.'

"I said I was sorry. But for Briggs, saying sorry was bullshit."

RIVER

I know I'm just telling the story to Jillian, but it comes back at me so hard it's like I'm reliving it.

"You're sorry?" Briggs had said, acting surprised. "What are you sorry for?"

I didn't know how to answer. I wasn't sorry for anything. I hated him more than I had ever hated anyone. All I was sorry for was playing football and ever meeting him.

Like an asshole, I said, "I want to write plays," as if I had to give him an explanation. Before I knew what was happening, he turned me around and slammed me against the locker, pressing a baseball bat against the back of my neck.

"You are not quitting the team," he said through his gritted teeth. "Do you hear me? You are going to finish out the year and come back next year, and you are going to keep us in first place because that's what you're here for. That's why you exist." Those were his exact words. *That's why you exist.*

I winced from the impact, not knowing what to do. My first instinct was to fight him, to kill him, but something told me to freeze so he'd get off me.

"Did you hear me?" he said.

"I heard you," I said. Then he threw me to the ground, took his belt off and hit me with it. I wasn't wearing a shirt and the buckle slit my back open. I nearly blacked out.

"*Sir*," he said.

Then before he left the locker room he said, "You will stay on the team and play better than you ever have in your life because if you don't I will ruin you and your friend, Ryan. Do you understand?"

I didn't answer, and he swung his belt at me again.

"Yes, *sir*," he said.

JILLIAN

River stops. I don't know if I can breathe.

"Now you know where the scar came from," he says. "I got twenty stitches at the emergency room. They asked me what happened...I said I got mugged and they told me to file a police report. I knew they suspected something, but I got out of there fast."

I want to say something, anything, to comfort him, to ease the pain, but I can't. "Did you tell anyone?"

He looks away before he answers, as if he's going over it in his head. He opens his mouth as if to say something, and then he shakes his head.

"What then?" I ask him.

He shrugs. "I did the only thing that would get to him."

"What?"

"I started the fire."

"Why?"

"To ruin him."

"You mean to burn his records, all his game plans?" Everyone knew

222

Briggs kept game plans about every game he ever coached. He was fanatical about taking notes, recording every detail. Maybe he was going to write a book or his memoir.

"It wasn't that," River says. "That's what everyone thought."

"Then what?"

"He kept something else, I found out."

"What?"

"Profiles of every kid who ever played on his teams. I was in his office one day when he was out on the field, and I opened the file drawers to see what he had in there. He detailed everything he could find out about all of us, from our strengths in the game to our weaknesses."

"Why?"

"To control us. But that wasn't all. He found out about our private lives too."

I hold my breath.

"He knew how my mom died and where," River says. "He had her obit in his file. He had my transcripts and all the articles about me from the school paper. He even knew who I dated and where I hung out. There were pictures of Lexie and me. Even reports from a shrink she went to and accusations of bullying against her that came into the guidance office. I had no idea about any of it."

"That's so creepy."

"It gets worse. The biggest file was about Ryan. Stuff about his jobs, modeling pictures, a list of the bars where he hung out—even pictures of different guys he was with."

"Did he ever use any of that against anyone?"

"I'm sure he would have if he thought it would help him. Briggs is sick, obsessive about every detail."

"Know the enemy," I say.

"Or your team."

"Did anyone else know?"

He shrugs. "So I burned it all to gut him, to gut his power."

"How did they know it was you?"

"He told them."

"He wasn't afraid?"

"You think anyone would believe me over him?"

"So the school called the cops?"

"About an hour after the fire. Briggs told them I missed practices and that I was late too often. He said I was on drugs. He gave them the coke from my locker as proof with my fingerprints on it. That was all they needed. Briggs said he held it because he wanted to give me a second chance, that he had high hopes for me. But he said I was furious when he told me he was going to kick me off the team." He shakes his head. "They brought me before a corrupt judge, and that was it, never mind my side of it."

"But how come nothing ever came out?"

"The school hushed it up. It was so ugly, they just wanted it to be over. No publicity. No nothing."

He crosses his arms over his chest, hugging himself, his head down. It looks like all the energy and fight are drained out of him now. He closes his eyes, exhausted.

CHAPTER 30

RIVER

I have to get out of here.

We leave Briggs's office and go back to the theater, up on the stage to stay dry. We stay up all night going over it. How my life changed after that. About Briggs. I never thought I'd tell anyone, only when I started talking to her, I couldn't stop. She cared. She saw the me that no one else did anymore.

It's still raining, but the wind is quieter, as if the storm is running out of energy. We're stretched out behind the dark curtains, hidden away.

"Remember Prometheus?" Jillian says.

"That was my term paper."

"Fire was his gift to humanity," she says.

"Right, and they chained him up and every day an eagle ate his liver."

"But it grew back," she says.

"Yeah, until the next day when it happened again."

"But he was freed," she says.

"Eventually, in some versions."

We talk about all the things I could or should have done differently. About being wronged with the whole world believing a lie that takes on a life of its own. And no one giving you a chance.

By two in the morning we burn out, fantasizing that by getting out the truth, you can heal, like washing dirt out of an infected wound and then stitching it up. But wounds leave scars, and I have them inside and out.

In spite of the damage around us, in spite of me telling the story I had replayed a million times in my head, but vowed never to speak of—or maybe because of all that—we fall dead asleep in each other's arms for what seems like a lifetime.

• • •

I sense that something's different before I even open my eyes. The chaos outside has been replaced by calm. I stand up and go over to the windows in the theater, pulling back the curtains.

Overnight, the world has been reborn.

There's brilliant sunshine for the first time in forty-eight hours. All the destruction that surrounds us is now bathed deceptively in a golden light. I stare at the sky and question my sanity. Did it really happen? How could everything change so much overnight?

It's hard to understand what I'm seeing. Jillian gets up and we climb up on a second floor windowsill and stare out at demolished homes, downed power lines, toppled trees, garbage, furniture, roof shingles, and worst of all dead animals—lots of them now, birds, cats, and dogs—floating along as calmly as if they're asleep. And beneath the surface of the water probably snakes, all kinds of them.

"We can't go outside or we'll get electrocuted. The power lines are all close to the ground now."

"Someone will come around here and find us," Jillian says. "Or there will be helicopters flying over us. If we can get onto a windowsill, they'll see us." She stares off into the distance, and then turns back to me. "When life starts again, you have to talk to Ryan and convince him to go to the police. Briggs can't get away with what he did."

"The school heads don't want shit raining down on them," I say. "They won't want to admit what happened. What they believe is that I set the fire. Kids could have gotten killed."

JILLIAN

I stop and it hits me. Secrets. We had been telling each other our deepest secrets, but River was still keeping the hardest one inside him.

"Believe?"

"What?" he says, looking confused.

"You said, 'What they believe is that I set the fire.'"

He turns away.

"River..." I grip his arm. "You didn't do it, did you?"

He doesn't answer.

"The truth matters—please."

"It's too late."

"It isn't!"

"I paid for it," he says. "I lost almost four months of my goddamn life, not to mention half my brain and my sanity. I thought I'd get a few weeks, maybe a month at most and then they'd spring me. Only it didn't work that way."

"It was Ryan, wasn't it? He set the fire and you took the blame."

He looks at me and turns away.

"Why? Why would you do that, River?"

"He was so broken," he says, his voice cracking. "You know what he went through. I couldn't let anything else happen to him. He would have killed himself, and it would have been my fault. I tried to get him to tell them, but he wouldn't. There was no other way."

"You have to tell at some point. You have to report him."

"At some point," he says robotically. "If anyone cares."

"You were locked up for no reason, and Briggs has to be stopped."

"It's over now; it's too late. You think anyone will really care?"

"We'll make them care. We have to," I urge.

"Bullshit." River looks around like he's reliving it. "You want to hear something really crazy?"

"What?"

"You know what I still think about sometimes?"

"What?"

"The canary, Briggs's canary."

"What do you mean?"

"Before the fire Ryan put the cage near the window and opened the door. The tiny bird stood there for a few seconds as if he was thinking about it, like he was weighing his options. Then he went out, he flew away. Ryan knew he would. He wanted that helpless thing to escape from Briggs, whatever the cost."

"Yeah?" I say.

"I keep wondering whether the poor bird survived."

• • •

Time stands still. A wide oasis of silence surrounds us under the cornflower-blue sky. There's no wind, no motion. The only things we see stirring are the mosquitos feasting on the garbage outside.

We wait inside where it's safe. There's nothing else to do. Someone will pass by. Someone will check on the school or the streets around it. It's just a matter of time. We perch ourselves on a windowsill in a second-floor science room.

River reaches for my hand and holds it in his. He's in pain from his shoulder, his face strained, his jaw tight, but he manages to stay calm. Both of us are filled with the same sense of relief. It's over, and we survived. Only I can't help asking myself, why? What obscure toss of the dice in the universe decided we would make it when so many others lost their lives?

• • •

EMS workers in trucks arrive, floodwater covering their tires. They pull up to the school. Two men get out. Am I seeing a mirage? We call out to them and they make their way to the school door, carefully stepping around the downed wires, brushing away the mosquitos and flies swarming over the stagnant pools of water surrounding us.

"What the hell," one of them says. "How did you get in here?"

"It's a long story," I say.

We go outside with him and climb into the truck. "How are you? You need medical care?"

"My shoulder…it's broken," River says.

"Was there anyone else inside with you?"

River looks off momentarily and then back at him. "No," we answer at the same time.

The EMT hands us water bottles and we drain them. "I have a sat phone," he says, handing it to me. "Try your parents."

• • •

I was almost eight when it happened. I remember because it was before my dad left. It was storming outside, there was thunder and lightning. We were staying at a house we rented in Maine for part of the summer. Our dog, Bree, was always scared of storms. It was too bad outside to walk her so we put her into the backyard to go. We waited for a few minutes to give her time, but when we called her, she didn't come back. Bree was trained, she always came when we called her, so we got concerned.

All of us went outside to look for her. We thought that maybe she ducked under a bush to hide from the storm, but she wasn't anywhere. Then Ethan shouted.

"The backyard gate. It's open!"

The guy who cut the grass had been there in the morning, and we realized he had forgotten to lock it behind him. We got into the car and drove around the neighborhood, shouting her name from the window. We called her again and again, but we couldn't find her. We must have been driving around searching for an hour when my dad suddenly stopped short.

Bree was running across the road.

If he hadn't stopped in time, he would have hit her. He ran out and called her name and she stopped. He carried her into the backseat and all of us started crying, happiness mixed with relief.

That scene comes back to me now as the phone rings and rings and finally, I hear her voice. The connection is full of static. It sounds like she's a million miles away, or at the bottom of a well. But it's her, it's my mom. She's alive. She's OK.

"Mom?" It's hard to breathe.

"Jilly?"

That was what she called me when I was growing up. "Yeah, mom," I finally answer, my voice cracking. I hear a stifled sob.

"Oh my God, honey." Her voice breaks. She can't go on.

Then I hear Ethan's voice. "Jill?" He takes the phone from my mom. They must have found each other.

"You know how scared we were?" he says. "Jesus Christ!" And then silence before I hear something I've never heard before—my brother sobbing too.

"It's OK, Ethan," I whisper. "It's OK." I cradle the phone against my heart, waiting for him to stop.

River takes the phone after me. He dials his dad's cell number and waits. No answer, not that it surprises us. He hits end and stares off into the distance. A grimace of pain washes over his face.

I reach for his hand, slipping my fingers through his, holding tight. He squeezes my hand back, then stares ahead, biting the side of his lip.

• • •

My mom is staying at a hotel in downtown Houston, and I meet her there. Ethan is with her. He came back as soon as the storm ended, staying downtown in a hotel where Jerry's dad worked.

River comes with me while city workers try to contact local hospitals and aid workers to find his dad. We get to my mom's room, but she and Ethan must have gone outside, so we go inside and watch the news while we wait.

"Much of the highway traffic was hit dead on by the hurricane," the reporter says. "Cars were lifted and sent flying. Thousands were killed. We don't have a final count of the dead. That could take weeks."

The TV shows aerial views of people on rooftops waiting to be rescued and highways submerged in water. It looks like a topsy-turvy world of water. Streets have been turned into giant bayous with trees and light poles sticking out of the water at odd angles.

There's an interview with the mayor, who's wearing an open shirt with the sleeves rolled up. His eyes are half closed, like he hasn't slept in days.

"All that the police, firefighters, and city officials care about right now is cutting losses and saving people before it's too late," he says. "But it's a huge city and the devastation is everywhere. People are trapped in houses, buildings, and cars, slowly dying of thirst and starvation. They need help fast, and fortunately we've gotten calls from EMS workers and firemen throughout the country who are making their way here to help us."

The camera switches to aerial footage of the city again, and a voice-over provides a running commentary: "Bodies are everywhere, stuck in attics where people ran to avoid floods below, and in hospitals that ran out of food, oxygen, and medication. Corpses are on the streets too, floating in the floodwaters, flesh decomposing, giving off the stench of rotten eggs. The bodies are everywhere, left behind like soldiers on a battlefield. Only these victims were defenseless."

Looting is widespread, the report says. There are unconfirmed reports about drug addicts going into hospitals and shooting nurses in the head in their desperate efforts to find drugs.

And the people left standing, the ones we see on the streets who were spared, look numb and in shock.

We want to turn the TV off, but we can't look away. We're speechless, unable to move, tears blurring our vision.

Nothing in this city will ever be the same again.

CHAPTER 31

THREE WEEKS LATER

RIVER

The National Guard was called in. Volunteers from across the country came to help put life back together. The bodies are being buried. There are funerals. Every day.

My dad survived. Turned out that the marine corps sticker on his car helped save his life. After sitting in gridlock for hours after we left, he got off the highway. He came looking for us, but the storm got worse and he had to give up. He searched frantically for shelter, going to building after building, and finally, after pounding on the side of a warehouse door where he heard sounds, someone answered. The guy inside was a former marine too, and he took my dad in.

After it was over though, he spent a couple of weeks in an over-crowded, understaffed hospital. Dehydration, broken ribs, and some weird blood infection that nearly killed him. All the names of hospital patients were listed on a registry they printed in the newspaper. I went to see him three weeks after we left the school.

• • •

I open the door to his hospital room and stand still.

"Go ahead," says a nurse passing by. "It's fine."

I'm not sure it is. I nod to her and take a step in. He's sharing the room with two other men. One of the beds has gauzy white curtains drawn around it. A second holds a man with an IV in his arm. I figure my dad is in the bed near the window, only his face is turned away, so I can't see it.

I feel off balance, like the earth is vibrating under my feet. I need something to hold on to. I hate hospitals, everything about them—the smells, the staff people who don't meet your eyes, the look of the place—all of it, ever since...

I walk over to his bed and grab the cold handrail to steady myself. He's sleeping. He's almost yellow, his eyes sunken, the creases across his forehead deeper than I remember. His lips are dried, cracked. He looks broken down, almost lifeless.

"Dad?" I whisper.

After a few seconds, his eyes flicker and then open. He turns to me, a look of shock on his face.

"River!"

I can't make out his expression. Disbelief? Despair? I see a sudden flash of anger in his eyes.

"You just ran..." he says, and then as quickly the anger vanishes. "But you made it." He shakes his head. "You outran it."

I never thought I'd see my dad break down. I drop to my knees, still gripping the railing. "It's OK, Dad, don't cry."

"I didn't know what to think. What could have happened. You just ran and..." His voice breaks.

I reach over and put my hand over his. He grabs it and holds it tightly. I look at him, not knowing what else to say. I think about all the conversations we never had. All the memories I should have, but don't, and it scares me because so many years have gone by like this. There's only this emptiness to look back on. We never talk about anything important. Anything real. Part of me feels like I'm looking at a stranger.

"I left the car, I tried to go after you, but I got caught in the storm. I wanted to help. To save you," he says. "But it got worse so fast."

"It's over, it doesn't matter now."

"It does matter," he insists. "I couldn't lose everything again…"

"You mean after Mom?"

"After you were taken away, in detention. And then with the storm coming. I tried to protect you, but I drove you away. I couldn't admit I was wrong. I turned my own son into the enemy for God's sake." A deep wail breaks from his throat.

"I'm here, Dad, please."

He looks up at me, meeting my gaze, and I hear something I've never heard him say before.

"I'm sorry. I'm so sorry, son."

I look away. All the feelings I didn't know were inside me, that I didn't know existed at all, pour out uncontrollably.

• • •

My dad comes home a week later. We sit down and I tell him everything that happened with Briggs. He doesn't say a word; he just listens. But it's more than listening. I see something in his eyes I've never seen before. Compassion. In my entire life I've never seen that in him. He takes three months off from work after that.

"We'll get Briggs put away," he says, "and clear your name. No matter what it takes." I see the marine in him again. The strength, the focus. The dedication to getting the job done. For the first time in my life, I like that.

That same week I get a text from Ryan: My dad died during the storm.

He's on his own now, orphaned overnight. No mom, no dad, just an aunt and uncle living in another part of the state.

Ryan and I meet and talk about everything that happened during the storm—and before, with Briggs.

"I tried to get into the school," he says. "I tried the key, but it didn't work, then I pounded on the door in case someone was inside, but it was useless." He held his hands out helplessly. "So I drove to a friend's house—a brick house—and we stayed there. But my dad was so scared and so shaken up he died of a heart attack."

Now I knew what the lights we saw were. But the noise of the hurricane blocked out their voices and the sound of him pounding on the door. If only we knew. I still have my dad, but his is gone and Ryan is more alone than ever.

"We have to stop Briggs," I say.

"It's going to be hard," he says, looking away. "Talking about it, telling everybody. I don't know if…"

"It's harder keeping it inside, torturing ourselves, acting like it didn't happen."

He stares off and then turns back to me finally. "I'm with you. I'll do whatever I have to."

"We'll get through it, no matter what, Ryan."

"Yeah," he says, his eyes filling with tears. I grab him and hug him, holding him while he leans against me crying.

SIX WEEKS LATER

Together with my dad and Jillian's mom, we go to the school authorities. And then the District Attorney. They ask us a million questions and tape our stories. We tell them everything we know and everything we found.

They promise to be in touch.

"There will be a long investigation," Jillian's mom says. "They'll contact the schools Briggs worked in before. But in the meantime, the school is forcing him to take a leave. The paper will stay on top of it," she says, "until we get him locked up."

Once people start asking questions, word begins to spread. One morning before school starts, Jillian's mom gets a call at home. It's someone who works in the school. Someone who won't give her name. But she's someone who can't stand by and do nothing while the truth gets buried.

"We were cleaning up after the storm and we found files," the woman told her. "They were inside the burned-out file cabinets in Briggs's office. There were a lot of damaged files, but we were able to piece together some of the papers, and we saw the records Briggs was keeping on all the players. We knew he crossed the line. There were photographs of one of the players in a car with another boy. Pictures like that have no place in the office of a football coach," she said. "It set off alarm bells."

"My mom's meeting with the woman in a restaurant out of town," Jillian tells me. "My mom convinced her to bring copies of the files with her, so she'll have the evidence firsthand."

A few days after the meeting, her mom called the principal. He agreed to sit down and talk with her.

"I guess he was ambushed," I say. "There's no way he can be in denial any longer."

After their meeting, we hear that the principal met with the school board and they agreed to cooperate.

One of the gym teachers has taken over as coach. For the first time in over a year, I feel a sense of hope.

I leave my job and after my shoulder starts to heal, I spend my time fixing up our house. There's an endless amount of work to do, but the workers are happy to have an extra guy and they're willing to teach me. Building is therapeutic, and it beats shelving groceries.

Our house has damage inside and out and when I'm not working on it, I help the guys fixing Jillian's. Their roof has to be replaced, and there's lots of damage to the outside walls. But at least we both have homes. They're still standing.

The local paper runs a story about all the dogs left homeless by the storm. I leave it on the kitchen table that morning.

"Go down there," my dad says. That's it. I don't need any more encouragement.

• • •

"How do we even start?" Jillian says, walking up and down the aisles of what looks more like a concrete bunker than a shelter, looking at dog after dog, every one of them anxious and scared, their loud, desperate barking ricocheting off the walls to command our attention.

"Find the one that looks the most pathetic," I say. It doesn't take long.

I stop in front of a cage and see a dog at the far end, huddled against the windowless back wall, as close as she can get, her head drooping, fixed on the floor. She's a ball of tangled, matted black fur, maybe fifty pounds. Lab mixed with something. Terrier maybe. Her whole body is quaking with fear. I recognize things in her I see in myself: pain, hurt, resignation, isolation. I kneel down and wait outside the bars of the cage. I know she senses that I'm there, but she doesn't move.

"Can you take this one out?" I call to a guy who works there. "Can I walk her?" He comes over and unlocks the cage door and reaches in and puts a collar around her neck. "Sad case," he says.

We take her for a walk and after a few minutes she stops and looks up at me, her chocolate eyes sizing me up, unsure. I kneel down and rub her head and talk to her softly. I feed her a biscuit, then another one. She leans against me, pushing as close to me now as she was to the concrete wall of her cage. That's it. She's not homeless anymore.

She has a home now. Mine.

We name her Dawn.

THREE MONTHS LATER

JILLIAN

We go back to school three months after the storm. The school board set up off-site classrooms. Some of my friends made it through Danielle. Some didn't.

Kelly and her family disappeared, like they never existed. Something like that doesn't seem possible. It's something I can't begin to process. There's no information yet on what happened to them. We don't know what happened to her family's car. All we have are questions. Are their bodies out near the highway somewhere? Did their car get swept someplace else?

So many bodies haven't been identified yet. The cleanup is far from over. Corpses still turn up floating in the sewage-clogged water. It's so savage. So unthinkable. It will take months, maybe years to find all the missing. To track down the dead. Or maybe we'll never know.

I can't accept it. I can't and never will. I want to ask Kelly things. I want to go to her for advice. I want to hang out with her and go places, do fun things, stupid things. I still anticipate the way she would answer the questions I would ask, that sure-of-herself style—no matter what the topic, as if she knew everything, dressed in the latest fad stuff, "too cool for school."

Kelly never worried about stuff that scared the rest of us. Failing tests. Getting into college. Getting guys to like you. And especially really scary things—like hurricanes.

She was my best friend, and now I don't have her. She's not anywhere and that just makes no sense to me. It's stupid, I know, but I keep dialing her cell number, waiting for her to pick up on the other end.

And her picture.

The one of her in her pink bikini and floppy hat, the one that I took in Galveston when the surf was calm, and I captured one of life's rare and perfect moments. I stare at it hard as though in some way—wherever she is now—my thoughts can reach her and she'll know I'm thinking about her and everything we shared. I need to keep doing that. To hold on to that. To remind me that's what life really is, odd collages of those isolated, perfect, beautiful shared moments with people you love. That's the best you can hope for. That's all we have to hold on to, to keep inside ourselves, no matter what.

"I keep telling myself that up until the end, she probably never allowed herself to think it was over," I say to Sari. "I doubt it ever occurred to her there was nothing she could do to stop Danielle. She probably never realized it was her time to go, never allowed for the possibility."

"She was all about living," Sari says. "Every day, every crazy minute. She was a hundred percent alive, a hundred percent with you."

Only now she's not. She's gone, reduced to a memory.

• • •

We talk about her less and less because it's too hard to look back. Her dad, a surgeon at Memorial, her mom, a pediatric nurse, two brothers, Mike and Quinn. All of them gone now like they were never born, like so many of the people on that highway who stayed where they were because they thought there was literally nowhere to turn. I can't come to terms with it. I doubt I ever will. All I know is the pain and the sadness, as I relive the memories of what happened during the storm and after, again and again and it rubs me raw inside.

So many of the after-effects of the storm are buried within us.

A psychiatrist on TV called it post-traumatic stress disorder. I never went to war, I never pulled the trigger of a gun, but I imagine this is what soldiers go through because none of us can get over seeing so much death around us.

I try to focus on moving on. I don't talk to Aidan anymore. He knows I'm seeing River. He also knows what he did, helping Lexie get River's combination. Maybe he didn't know how bad it was. Maybe he didn't know what he was paving the way for. But he did it, and I don't think he cared how badly it could hurt River. Aidan was like that. Single-minded. About basketball. About everything.

I think of all the things that were missing between us, but what I see most now is the emptiness.

Lexie got punished by the storm too, but what she lost was something she could get past. She and her parents survived, but their home was totally destroyed. They were forced to move in with her aunt in a house in a suburb of Dallas. No one knows if she's ever coming back. She tried to call River a few times, he told me. She left messages saying she was frantic to know how he was. He ignored the calls.

• • •

River and I run together three times a week. I can now go between three or four miles without getting winded, but he goes ten. We also do laps in our pool. He has weights and he's put me on a weight-lifting program.

"So you'll be able to outrun the next category five hurricane," he says, his smirky smile on his face more days than not.

When I look at him now, I can't help thinking of a quote I read: "Sometimes you put up walls not to keep people out, but to see who cares enough to break them down."

That's the first entry in my new diary, the one I bought for my post-Danielle life. This one doesn't include the "suckworthy dad" section. He's not mentioned at all. I'm working on letting go of the anger because

I won't be a victim to it anymore. That's a decision that's mine to make, I realize now.

I read a quote about forgiveness being an evolution of the heart. It makes me stop and think of how living through Danielle and surviving it changed me inside. The death and destruction from the storm was everywhere, but at some point you need to focus more on rebuilding and moving forward than on looking back. It's your choice to be a victim of the past. Or not to be.

And that gives me a new direction.

I want to be the person who breaks down walls and gets to the truth. If I can find a newspaper to hire me after I finish college, that's what I want to do.

• • •

River's moving on too. He's seeing a new therapist now, someone he says he can really talk to.

"The guy spends his nights playing in a band," River says, smirking. "I saw them on YouTube; they're not bad."

And for the first time, River's thinking about what he wants to do with his life too, looking forward more than back. My mom is convinced we can get his record expunged, clearing the way for him to finish his last year and a half of high school and then go to college.

• • •

Because of all the water damage around the house, we have cartons and cartons of books and files to sort through. One night River and I are looking through a stack of books from a bookcase in the den in my house. Some of them were damaged by dampness, but most of them are OK. There's an art book with a section on Japanese art and a tradition called kintsugi, a way of repairing broken pottery, usually with gold.

"I love this," I say. "You fix the damage, you refine it, but you don't hide it."

"Never heard of it," he says.

I look at a before-and-after picture of a cup with a deep crack in it. In the after picture, the crack is outlined in gold. It looks like a design element, not an attempt at repairing it.

"You use lacquer dusted with gold, silver, or platinum to repair the cracks," I read. "The damage isn't hidden, it's enhanced, giving the piece more character."

I look at River and think of all he's gone through, and what he's still going through. None of that will ever disappear or be forgotten. But maybe he'll grow better for it in some way—using it to reach out and help others. Or creating art by drawing on the damage inside him, not pretending it doesn't exist anymore.

I don't say any of that, but he looks at me. He gets it.

"Cool," he says.

Eventually we go outside to the pool, dangling our feet in the water. The air is still, perfumed by jasmine. There's a full moon and a sprinkling of stars in the sky.

The fence between our houses was torn up, most of the bushes uprooted. Eventually we'll get around to replacing the boxwoods and putting in a new fence, but in the meantime, there's no divide between River's backyard and mine anymore.

"No fences between us," he says, slipping his arm around my waist. "I like it this way."

I stare back at him, his blond-brown curls nearly reaching his tanned shoulders, his eyes glinting again with laughter. My heart beats harder, the love at category five now.

"So do I," I answer.

AUTHOR'S NOTE

Hurricane Kiss was inspired by a real-life encounter with a terrifying storm that threatened coastal Texas in September 2005. As Hurricane Rita barreled in, I was living in Houston with my husband, Ralph, and fifteen-year-old daughter, Sophie. Ralph, a reporter, was staying behind to cover the storm for the *New York Times*, while I was rushing to evacuate with Sophie, our dog and cat, and several hundred thousand other Houstonians.

We had reason to panic—less than a month before, Katrina had flooded New Orleans, killing close to 2,000 people. My husband had been one of the first reporters on the scene to witness the devastation.

Would Rita be another Katrina? Would it hit us dead on? We weren't waiting to find out. We hastily boarded up our windows with plywood. I packed the car with essentials and joined the exodus, heading for an inland town near Austin where we thought we'd be safe.

But like River and Jillian, we didn't get far—poor planning had gridlocked the escape routes. It took us close to seven hours to crawl less than twenty miles, and the traffic jam we were trapped in extended for a hundred miles. If the hurricane hit at that moment, I thought, we'd all be killed in our cars. I made a risky call: the highway back to Houston was empty. Surely we could find safety somewhere. I spun the car around and headed back.

We spent the night with hundreds of other evacuees and their dogs and cats in the ballroom of a downtown Houston hotel that welcomed pets. Then overnight, a miracle! Rita had veered off. The city had gotten a slap of wind and rain but escaped a knockout punch. A day later we headed home. Our house had been spared.

But I was haunted by what could have been. Fate spared us, unlike the victims of Katrina. That's why this book is dedicated to them.

Don't Miss These Great Reads from Deborah Blumenthal!

HC 978-0-8075-4535-5 $16.99 • PB 978-0-8075-4536-2 $9.99

An unforgettable summer of obsession, discovery, and miracles.

"A touching love story with just a hint of
magic and mysticism."—*VOYA*

Gia's family has plenty of secrets, but now she has secrets of her own...

"The twinkling backdrop of Manhattan and the budding romance between two opposites will make YA fans adore this novel."
—*RT Book Reviews*

HC 978-0-8075-4911-7 $16.99
PB 978-0-8075-4913-1 $9.99

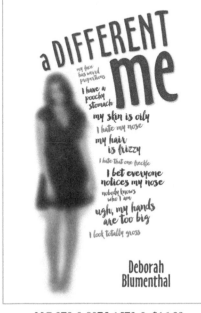

For Allie, changing her face has always been a secret wish...

"Allie struggles with her parents, her friends, and her self-esteem, and she becomes a stronger person for it."
—*School Library Journal*

HC 978-0-8075-1573-0 $16.99
PB 978-0-8075-1575-4 $9.99